Rednecks and Roses

By

Recycled Teenagers

ISBN: 0-7596-9880-5 (Ebook)
ISBN: 0-7596-9881-3 (Softcover)

This book is printed on acid free paper.

1stBooks – rev. 04/22/02

Table of Contents

Spradlin Hollow Baptizing

Bart Country

My Mama always said, "There's no such thing as a good snake. They're all just the same as the devil and all you got to do is look in the Bible; from the very beginning, it was a snake that was sent to tempt people.

Well, now, I'm almost ready to believe she's right; especially after what happened at the baptizing following our great revival meeting of July, 1937.

In the 1930's, Spradlin Hollow, Alabama, was an almost abandoned coal mining camp; and times were hard. Nobody there could afford a car, so the young people had to find their entertainment close to home. Attending church was one of the few ways for them to meet each other socially. Of course, there were the occasional wiener roasts or marshmallow toasts in the winter and watermelon cuttings in the summer. But going to church was the main thing; and a week long revival meeting was a big occasion—somewhere to go, every night for a week. Many couples became engaged in church, and not a few fell from Grace on the walk home afterwards.

July, the month for revival meetings in Spradlin Hollow is hot and humid. There was no air conditioning there in 1937, so the people kept cool in church by opening all the doors and windows and fanning themselves with cardboard fans-on-a-stick, supplied to all the churches by Brown Service Funeral Home.

Following the practice of generations of churchgoers, the Spradlin Hollow revivals were conducted with a set ritual: opening hymns sung by the congregation; a testimonial period, when anyone could stand and say what was in his heart or on his mind; a hymn sung while the offering was collected; the introduction of the visiting evangelist by the local pastor.

Then the evangelist delivered his sermon, after which he said a long fervent prayer seeking divine intervention for the saving of lost souls. The climax of the service was the invitation, when the preacher asked all to bow their heads while the congregation softly sang the invitation hymn—usually "Just as I am Without One Plea or "Softly

1

and Tenderly Jesus is Calling"—while his voice over-pleaded with sinners to come forward and be saved.

For the revival meeting in 1937, the evangelist was Brother Vernon Lee Willbanks, pastor of the near-by Sipsey Crossing Baptist Church—invited because of his record of many new members brought into the church and by his sincere and fiery sermons.

The first night's service was predictable; a satisfying message, enjoyable singing and two teen-aged girls came forward to accept the preacher's invitation—about what the congregation expected.

With each succeeding night the excitement mounted; the preacher became more animated; the hymn singing became louder and more people were coming forward to be saved. Friday night would be a night to remember—still remembered fifty-eight years later by all who were there and by those who said they were there.

That night was exceptionally hot and humid with storm clouds building and distant lightning flickering behind the hills in the west. The church was packed to overflowing; the crowd buzzing with anticipation, expecting something momentous. But what did happen was something no one would ever have predicted.

The church sat below a road that ran parallel to the east side of the building. The bank between the road and the church house provided a seat for those men who never went to church, but were entertained by the spectacle of a big and successful revival meeting.

That night they were joined by Doreen Sledge, a middle aged woman of something less than a virtuous reputation—a lot less. She was the sort of woman that mothers pointed out to their daughters with a warning: that's exactly what you expect to happen to women of easy virtue and alcoholic excesses.

Even those people who minded their own business and were liberal in their judgments were hard-pressed to find something good about her.

Doreen walked up to the men and said, "What the hell's all the excitement? ...No answer. "...anybody got a drink?"

There were a few grunts meaning, "No." "Well, at least, one of you bastards oughta have a smoke." One of the men handed her a can of Prince Albert tobacco and a pack of papers for her to roll her own; which she did as well as any man. Another gave her a match that she struck with her thumb nail.

There she was, a forty-two year old woman with dirty graying hair cut like a Dutch boy's; a greasy soiled dress that somebody gave her a long time ago; old tattered, run-down tennis shoes and squatting down on her haunches with a bunch of men no better than she was.

They treated her as their equal, so they accepted her as they did any of the men who were seated on the road-bank. The service had entered the invitation; the congregation was softly singing; the evangelist was calling for converts and something in Doreen's long forgotten past, something from her happy childhood moved her to tears. She stood up, scratched and started down the bank helped along by one man and then another, until she was standing in the opened back door to the church. She took a step inside the door. The amazed congregation on the front rows stopped singing. One by one the remainder stopped until the only one left singing was Miz Brakefield—singing alto with her eyes shut. She finally realized she was the only one singing, stopped and opened her eyes to see what was wrong.

Now, Doreen's moral turpitude was known area wide; even unto the Reverend Willbanks, who was rendered speechless by her dramatic entrance but soon recovered enough to take her to the altar for prayer. As she and the preacher knelt at the altar, there was a flash of lightning and a loud clap of thunder; the long delayed storm broke like the wrath of God There was hardly anybody in that church that did not think that God was making a statement. Everything that happened after that was anti-climactic.

There remained another night of revival but the people talked of nothing else except Doreen Sledge and her seemingly miraculous conversion. She was walking proof that God worked in marvelous ways, and all agreed that now indeed, they had seen everything. Because they had been privileged to see a once-in-a-lifetime miracle, many did not attend the last night of the revival. They did not expect anything to happen, so they went to the picture shows in Brookside instead.

The baptizing was scheduled for Sunday afternoon in Five Mile Creek, just above the bridge, where the water was waist deep and where there was easy access to the creek banks and a gentle slope down to the water. I was headed in that direction when I saw Benn

Gleason ambling along the road and called, "Hey Benn, whatcha doin'?"

"Aaa … just psyfoggin, around. Trying to make small-talk, I said, "Where you goin'?" "Goin' to the babsockey. Come and go with me.," Benn's language always was a mish-mash of humor, made-up words and controlled profanity. "I'm not about to miss that," I said.

When we arrived at the creek, both banks were lined with the righteous and the curious—the righteous to receive a blessing and the curious to see Doreen get baptized. Brother Hillhouse, the local pastor, was leading the singing of "Shall We Gather at the River" as one by one the converts were led into the creek by Brother Willbanks—one by one except for a young couple who had become engaged during the revival. They wanted to be baptized together, so Brother Hillhouse was recruited to help. The young couple went into the water holding hands, with Brother Hillhouse on one side and the evangelist on the other. As the couple came up out of the water, there was a scattering of applause from the creek banks.

Now it was Doreen's turn—what most people had come to see. Some good ladies in the church had bathed her, washed and brushed her hair and gave her a new print dress for the ceremonies.

Brother Willbanks led her cautiously into the creek, and they had taken a couple of steps when she stopped. Soothingly the evangelist said, "It's all right Sister Sledge. This will soon be over …and praise God … you will come out of the water a new creature."

She turned to him with a blank expression. He started to move forward but she held back. The preacher said, "Nothing to be afraid of Sister Sledge. We'll soon be finished. Amen." She said to him, speaking as though she was telling a universal truth, "There's a snake over there on that rock." Overwhelmed by the occasion and oblivious to what she was saying, the preacher again started for mid-stream, saying, "Won't be long now, Sister."

She jerked her arm out of his grasp, placed her hands on her hips, gave him a look that was designed to kill and said, "Goddammit, you dumb bastard, I said there's a goddam snake over there!"

From the crowd came nothing but total silence. The only sounds were the gentle rippling of the creek, a far off call of a blue-jay and a distant train blowing for a crossing in Adamsville.

Doreen Sledge stomped out of the creek and up the bank to where Benn and I were sitting. She paused, looked down at us and said, "Come on Brother Benn; let's get tuh hell outta here. I need me a beer."

Mr. Football

Bart Country

The young men who play football for the Muscle Shoals State University Raiders are very fortunate to have as their coach a man everybody calls Mr. Football. His name is Buford Football, and he is a legend in the Mid-South among those who follow Division II Sports. Coach Football is a taskmaster who demands perfection, and his players are a group of overachievers who love him and respond to his coaching with Herculean effort.

Their record for the last ten years is proof of this—135-5-0, eight conference championships, and four Division II national titles. Other coaches, who all are underpaid, supplement their incomes by signing lucrative contracts with equipment manufacturers and athletic shoe companies—but not Coach Football. He is as underpaid as the other coaches but he did not sign with Nike, Reeboks, Russell Manufacturing or any of that crowd. Rather, since his team is known as the Raiders, he signed a deal with Johnson Wax, the makers of RAID. He negotiated into his contract the added incentives of being paid a bonus of $100 each time he mentions RAID during an interview and it gets printed or broadcast. A further incentive is a $1000 bonus if he can somehow get his picture in the paper or on television with a can of RAID.

Since Coach Football is also athletic director, he is responsible for the schedule and he had signed a home-and home agreement with most of the teams in this area who have insects for mascots, such as: The Delta City (Miss. A. I. Wasps', The West Memphis College Hornets, and the Bad, Bad Boll Weevils of Washita State in Louisiana. Just this year he signed for homecoming The Fighting Fleas of Martin Luther King University, a new school located at Wallace Ferry in South Alabama's Black Belt Region.

Playing these teams with insect mascots provides Coach Football with many opportunities during interviews to whip out a can of RAID, hold the can so the photographers can see the label, squirt a cloud of spray and say something like, "It's a raaaaid! This is the way were gonna zap the Hornets." That's how the school got its famous yell during every kickoff—an extended sssssssssssssssssss and then ZAP!, when toe meets leather.

Coach Football used another method to get RAID mentioned by the media—intentional controversy. Once, in an interview he said there were no Jews his team since they were more interested in grubbing for money. The Jewish community were up in arms. ACLU denounced him and a Rabbi in Birmingham castigated him in Temple Immamuel by saying that Nazism started that way and used the opportunity to compare him to Hitler. The University called a press conference in the gym with the president of the college, the vice-president, the University's Director of Media Relations and Coach Football, all wired for sound, sitting on the stage and facing a large contingent of newspaper, radio and television reporters.

The president made a statement apologizing for any misunderstanding, and then the coach was introduced by the Media Director. Coach Football began by rummaging in his coat pocket for his notes, and along with his papers he pulled out a small can of RAID and absentmindedly laid it on the table with the papers and read this prepared statement: "Remarks were taken out of context and misquoted. I have nothing but respect for Jewish people, and I admire the way they have struggled to overcome many adversities. What I really said was that the young Jewish men at this university are diligently applying themselves to their study of Money and Banking, and to uphold their high scholastic averages they couldn't take on the added burden and pressure of football."

He folded his piece of paper, put it in his coat pocket, picked up the can of Raid and, amid flashing cameras…spritzed an imaginary fly and strode off the stage, leaving the administrative people to answer the clamoring press.

Once after a game in which the Raiders had lost three fumbles, a very angry Coach Football told the reporters, "It's almost an impossibility for the Nee-g-ro runners on this team to carry the ball without showing-off…holding it out with one hand like a loaf of bread and struttin' around like a bunch of monkeys."

"Well, I'm here to tell you they are going to play football my way or never carry another ball for me. There'll be no more dancing around on my football field unless they're doing the boogie with the cheerleaders at the May Day May pole."

The following media earthquake registered 6.7 on the Richter scale…COACH FOOTBALL FINALLY GOES TOO FAR screamed a headline … another said, FOOTBALL PUTS FOOT IN MOUTH. While newspapers all over the South printed front page stories, most were not as lurid as these a headlines.

Black ministers, nationwide, denounced Coach Football from their pulpits, the SCLC called news conferences to demand his resignation, the Reverend Jessie Jackson came down and attended rallies and held a huge prayer meeting in Birmingham's Legion Field and CBS sent their top news team to cover the story.

The upshot of all this was Coach Football had many opportunities to say "RAID" for publication and four times he was pictured with a can of RAID —once on CBS. The university had no intention of firing him. Where else could they find a coach who won every game and worked so cheaply?

Coach Football's RAID promotion was made part of the homecoming celebrations; indeed, there were those detractors who maintained that it was the celebration. The theme for homecoming was: IT"S A RAID! SSSSSSSSSSSSSSS ZAP! The Johnson Wax Company sent some large banners and many cardboard signs printed with this slogan and showing a photograph of a huge can of RAID with sssses spraying from the nozzle. They also sent hundreds of dummy cans of RAID on sticks for the fans to wave around.

The winning fraternity/sorority house decoration featured a seven foot paper-mache can of RAID with a twenty foot long banner stapled to the nozzle and SSSSSS ZAP! printed across it to where a huge papier-mâché flea with X's for eyes was attached to a five-foot pole.

As game time neared, the festivities were transferred to the football stadium. The stands were almost filled when the Raiders came onto the field for their customary walk-around check of turf playing conditions and passed in front of the King University fans, who started their rhythmic chant.

The chant was begun by their band's tuba section, who played four-note tune from everybody's childhood: "My-dog-has-fleas" Then they made a chopping motion with their right arm and right hand—the hand curved into a claw—and chanted, "Scratch-Scratch-Scratch!— over and over the whole game long. Occasionally, the chant was interrupted for this yell:

Yo, Raiders!
Y'all gonna scratch
When it itches.
When we kick butts
Y'all mess in yo, britches!

Two o'clock arrived amid a cacophony of tubas, sssszap, scratch, scratch, scratch, and, only God knows why, a few "Roll-Tides' and a sprinkling of "War-Eagles" The crowd was in a frenzy as the coin was tossed, and the Raiders won the toss and elected to receive. The ball was teed up, ssssssssssssszap!, and it was airborne. Waiting at the goal line to receive was Tyrone Flatt, All-American wide receiver and kick returner—nick-named Ten Flatt, because he could run "the hundred" in ten seconds flat—in full uniform, carrying a football.

Having become angered by the constant taunts, "chops" and "scratches" of the King University fans, Ten Flatt turned toward their cheering section and gave their "chops" and "scratches" back at them. Alas, In doing so, he took his eyes off the ball for just a second. It hit him on the head, bounced straight up and fell at his feet on the one yard line, where he kicked it around and into the end-zone. Frantically he raced after the skittering ball and fell on it for a safety.

Coach Football, whose face was white with rage, yanked Tyrone off the field, shoved him onto the bench where he sat for the remainder of the game—in complete and inconsolable disgrace.

The Fleas never crossed mid-field again. The Raiders scored 77 unanswered points while amassing 810 yards of total offense—373 yards rushing and 437 yards passing.

Surely this awesome display of offensive power, the flawless defense, the huge margin of victory and, certainly, the many opportunities for him to say "RAID" would cause Coach Football to be well pleased. Never in hell—the other team had scored two points.

The Night the Church Went to the Bushes

Perry Woodly

My brothers and I and the Sherer boys were known as the boys from hell—Poley Hollow. Our neighbors had heard about the yellow-jackets that were released at that Pentecostal revival and they even went around saying that Bad-eye Sherer had lost his eye when he was stung by one of those yellow-jackets.

Our reputation in the Boldo community was not very good because the people there gave us credit for pranks that we were not involved in. In fact, we were working in the fields when most of the stunts were being pulled. The young ladies in our school were warned by their mothers to stay away from the boys in Boldo. As our reputation grew, so did our following.

Poley Creek and Poley Hollow lay between our place and the Sherer's property. When school was in session, during the winter months, my brothers and I would stop at the Sherer place to warm up and then walk the two miles to the bus stop.

One day, on our way home from school, we and the Sherer boys put our heads together and decided that we needed a club house. Bad-eye Sherer and my brother, Lent, scouted out the best places for the club house cabin that we were going to build up Poley Creek.

It was going to be a big secret, so only the club members would know the location. We spent all our spare time building the cabin, and by August we were ready to move in. During this time all our neighbors were complaining about missing chickens and watermelons. Now, believe me, we were being good boys—too good—for we were burnt out on fried chicken.

The first meeting was called on Saturday night, the second week in August. Somebody had brought a kerosene lamp and we sat around it smoking roll-your-own Country Gentleman cigarettes and coughing our fool heads off. At this meeting it was determined that we needed a neat name for our club and we decided that Poley War Hawks described us to a "T".

We worked out secret codes and handshakes, and boy, we went the whole nine miles on secrecy—the Masonic Lodge had nothing on us. Our families thought that we were into religion in a big way. They believed that we were going to all the revivals in the county, when in reality all our time was spent at the cabin thinking up new mischief to get into. Every since that famous yellow-jacket incident we didn't feel all that welcome at church. We were shunned.

The preacher's sermon was often about "spare the rod and spoil the child". When he delivered this sermon he always looked directly at us Poley War Hawks. This didn't seem fair to us, but we laid low and behaved ourselves so we could get back in the good graces of our neighbors.

One Saturday night after we had moved into our club house, the Pentecostal Holiness Church was going to have a box-supper and cake-walk. This made necessary a special meeting of the Poley War Hawks. We met and came to the conclusion that we had to do something to derail the supper.

Again, the yellow-jackets were brought up but they were quickly ruled out. As the Country Gentleman was passed around and as the cabin filled with Smoke, I came up with the idea of substituting Ex-Lax for the chocolate icing on the cakes. Everybody agreed that this was a good idea and we discussed how we could accomplish our mission.

Reluctantly, we decided that we would have to bring in the girls somehow. Some of the girls had been bugging us to join the War Hawks, so we agreed to make them Hawkettes.

Saturday night rolled around and we were pleased that the Hawkettes had outdone themselves—all the cakes were chocolate. They gave us the thumbs up and we were ready for the fun to begin, but we had no idea how long it would take for the Ex-Lax to kick in.

Soon the box-suppers and cakes were sold and eaten Reverend Grady gave thanks which lasted for an hour. When he got wound up the shouting and praising of the Lord went on for a long time.

As the service wore on people in the congregation started to hold their stomachs and began to edge toward the outhouse. Soon there was a stampede for the privy and a traffic jam formed at the toilet door causing the crowd to spill over into the bushes. Every bush had somebody behind it. They were in for a surprise because what they didn't know was the bushes were full of poison ivy.

11

As we hurried away from the church grounds we were doubled over with laughter. Bad-eye was missing. Somebody said that he had forgotten that the cakes had been doctored with Ex-lax and had eaten two big pieces. Lent said that the last time he saw him he was headed for the bushes.

The Reverend Gready, who now had more fuel for his sermon, said that the devil was working overtime and we'd better repent while there was still time. To this day only the War Hawks and Hawkettes know the truth about the night the church went to the bushes.

Rummy

Perry Woodley

The year of 1961 found me on my first tour of Vietnam. This was the first of my three tours. In 1961 the country was beautiful. The country hadn't been ravaged by war.

I was assigned to the 7th Special Forces to an A-team. The team was made up two officers and eight enlisted men. The men had been through the Special Forces school at Ft. Bragg, N.C. They were trained in guerilla warfare. The Special Forces were the elite forces of the Army; I was to be the team medic. The medic before me had committed suicide. I was leery of this old country boy going to such an elite outfit.

The Army sent our team to train a Vietnamese Ranger Battalion. The camp was in the middle of the jungle. The only way in was by chopper. The team landed at noon and we were met by the rangers who dressed in part civvies and fatigues. Most were barefoot. I thought hell, I have stepped in deep do…do.

Our team leader, Captain Bacon, called a meeting and said our first project was making a landing strip. Our living quarters were bamboo and straw hootches. The outhouse was a slit trench. Lieutenant Fogarty was assigned to build an outhouse while we were clearing the landing strip. As we went to work on the landing strip, I saw a snake as big as my leg slither into the jungle. Needless to say, I wasn't too hip about working in the Elephant grass. The grass came to our waist.

We finally finished the strip and planes were landing. We were to stock a hospital and get plenty of supplies. I ordered enough medical supplies and plenty of 190 alcohol. This I would use to sterilize my medical equipment plus the 190 made a good screwdriver.

Captain Bacon had already warned me that no booze was to be brought in with the supplies. In one week we had the dispensary up and running. I had a lot of cases of jungle rot. Most of the Rangers were infected with tape worms. The kids all had some type of skin disease. Captain Bacon said now I would have to take care of villagers. I was to visit two villages a week. The rangers would provide security.

Lieutenant Fogarty was in charge of base sanitation. He built the only outhouse that you had to go armed to sit on the throne. Fogarty got the bright idea of getting rid of the flies and smell at the outhouse. He poured five gallons of gas in the outhouse and using toilet paper for a fuse, he backed off about fifty feet. He completely forgot about the fumes from the gasoline that had followed him as he was getting the fuse ready. Fogarty lit the fuse and a big explosion followed. The outhouse went a hundred feet in the air. Human crap fell like rain drops. The Lieutenant had his eyebrows singed off. He came to my dispensary wanting medical treatment. I made him take a shower before I would treat him.

On one of my trips to the villager I bought a baby monkey from some kids. The monkey was real young. His eyes weren't open and he didn't have any hair. I brought him back to the dispensary and started feeding him crushed bananas and powdered milk. In one weeks time the monkey had his eyes open and he went everywhere I went. He rode on my aid kit.

When he had been with me three weeks, the monkey began to pick up some of my bad habits such as smoking and drinking my screwdrivers. I named him Rummy.

After six months in the jungle, we were getting a break. They were sending us to the South Vietnamese Military Academy as instructors. Some CIA man, who was our boss, said for us to take a week in Saigon. Said we would have to be straight when we got to Dalat where the school was.

It was party time for the team in Saigon. I got Rummy a set of fatigues. He went bar hopping with me. I told the bar girls that Rummy was a midget GI. Rummy got drunk one day and ran the maids out of our rooms. They refused to come in as long as Rummy was in the room.

Our week was up and Captain Bacon poured the team an the Goony bird that was taking us to Dalat. We were all sick on the trip except Rummy. When the Goony bird landed we were met by a band and a whole herd of Colonels. The Commanding officer gave us a welcoming speech.

When we were leaving to go to our new quarters, the Colonel came over and said that no pets were allowed. I was too sick to argue. Rummy sat on my shoulder and gave the Colonel the finger.

I couldn't believe my eyes when we got to our quarters. We had some rich Viet's summer Villa. Each man had his own room and there was a fully stocked bar. Bacon said the bar would stay locked until we got our job assignments. Captain Bacon left and Bartel shot off the lock. We partied the night through.

My job was to take care of the military and dependents. The dependents had it made - they had maids and house boys. They were damn snobs. In my first week, I was turned in for uniform violation and for having Rummy on my shoulder. Since we were working for the CIA, I wasn't worried about the Colonel. Hell, we could do anything short of murder and get away with it. The Colonel called me in and proceeded to chew my ass out. After his speech, I said, "Colonel, you can kiss where I can't and it isn't my elbow either."

When I arrived back at the house the team was out on the lawn. They informed me that Rummy was loose with a hand grenade. They didn't bother to open the windows when they left the building. They were pissed. They wanted to shoot Rummy, but there was a problem. They had left their weapons inside. I went to the door and looked inside. Rummy had the grenade that I had removed the powder from. The grenade was harmless. The team cheered when I came out with the grenade. I never told the team that the grenade was harmless.

Good Luck and Bad Luck

Woody

Bubba and Gator were sitting around the bar waiting for the lottery numbers to come up on TV. Bubba said "Gator, I feel it in my bones. We are going to hit it big. Just think twelve big ones. We can live high on the hog. Plenty of wine, women and song." "Yea, Bubba, you can have the women. I have Darlene who is all the women I can handle."

"Hey Suzie Q., Bring us another pitcher of beer, plus two more shots of redeye." "Damn it Gator, play it cool on the panther piss or we can't see the lottery numbers. If we win, we will get us a nascar. I shure like winston cup racing." "Gator, only rednecks go to stock car races. You know me I don't like for anyone to think I is a redneck. I have my reputation to protect."

"Hell, Bubba, why-do-you try and put on a big show? Yore family made moonshine and hunted gators in the swamp at old Mac Nut's place. Hell, you got drafted out of the third grade." "Gator you know I was sweet on Sally the teacher. That was the reason I stayed so long in the third grade. When my beard got too long some one turned me in to the Draft board. I had it made. I could whip everyone in the class. Made allstate playing basketball."

"Bubba were you the father of Sally Joe's baby? You know everyone thought you was." "Say Bubba, why do they have this T. V. preacher on before they give out the lottery numbers. Hell its old Oral. Ise calls him rectal. I can't stand the S.O.B. Guess I will have too listen, so I wont miss the lottery numbers. I have four tickets, so I'm bound to have the winner."

"Gator get out yore tickets out while I order us another round of rot gut they call whiskey. Hey Suzie? Two more shots. Make them doubles."

"Look Gator, the lottery girl is on. I hope she picks our numbers. Hey all you rednecks? Keep the noise down, Me and Gator are trying to concentrate. Here we go 11-13-20-9-4; hot damn, I have a winner. I can hardly breath or talk plus my chest hurts like hell. Gator, I think I'm having a heart attack.'

16

"Bubba you is only drunk, you aren't having a heart attack. Hey get off the floor. Hey Suzie, call 911, hurry, Bubba is dying. Hang on, Bubba. We have them Para-Medics on the way. What rotten damn luck. Win the big one and have a heart attack."

Suzie moved the onlookers away from Bubba and started mouth to mouth. The ambulance arrived and rushed Bubba to the hospital emergency room. The Doctors, after running many test on Bubba, decided that he had a bad case of indigestion and sent Bubba home.

Since the bar had closed, Bubba and Gator would be there first thing when the bar open to pick up their winning ticket.

Two weeks later, Bubba and Gator were sitting at the bar drowning their sorrows with beer and rot gut whiskey. Bubba asked the bar keep where Suzie and Stumpy had got off to. "Haven't you heard - Stumpy hit the lottery. Him and Suzie eloped and got married."

Bubba yelled "I'm having the big one. Don't call an ambulance, just let me die in peace."

Stump and Suzie bought the bar and named it the Lucky Lotto. They had twin boys who they named Bubba and Gator and lived happily ever after.

The moral of this story is: One man's garbage is another man's treasure.

Bubba goes Berserk

Woody

The music was of redneck vintage coming from the juke box at the Lucky Lotto, Bubba was drowning his sorrows with beer and whiskey. Bubba asked Suzie why she had barred Gator from the bar?

Suzie said Gator was drinking and cussing too much. "Hell, Gator's bar bill is over five hundred dollars. I won't let my mother run her bill that high. I run a bar not a charity. Bubba why don't you talk to Gator and get him to pay his bar bill and I will treat you nice."

"Suzie, you know that Gator has gone and hooked up with that NASCAR bunch. Hell they ain't nothing but hill billies. They is married to them cars. Hell, he has quit drinking and chasing women. Gator is still mad as a wet hen at you and Stumpy, cause you all got his lottery ticket. He should be like me, I don't have a jealous bone in my body. Suzie, I need me another beer and some quarters for the juke box. Say who is that blond bomb shell over there in that booth?"

"She said her name was Georgia. I figure that's short for Georgianna. She is down from New Orleans way. She shore has a lot of jewelry, she is lit up like a Xmas tree. Bubba if you are going to make a move an her, you had better do it before the mill hands get here. Today is payday and they come in here and let it all hang out."

"I guess you are right Suzie." "Hey" How do you like my boots and hat?"

"Bubba you look good but yore after shave would gag a maggot. Go wash off that smell and I will lend you some I bought Stumpy. Its the best. I spilt some on my poodle and my yard had fifteen female poodles. My poodle is named Princess."

Bubba went and washed off his after shave lotion, came back and yelled for Suzie to bring on her magic potent. "I am ready for some fun tonight."

"Here Bubba, just a dab will do you. I don't won't you using too much, I don't want the girls from the mill fighting over yore body." "Suzie, I am going to make my move. Bring us a couple of brews over to the booth."

Bubba strolled or shuffled over to the booth where Georgia sat, and said "What is a classy dame like you doing in a joint like this? My name is Bubba and can I buy you a drink?"

"Sure, Bubba, sit and tell me about yore self and this beautiful town. My Pappy left me some money when he died, I am looking for a place to call home. I like what I see, the men are big and strong and friendly."

"Georgia, we are friendly and nice people. I guess Suzie told you that I played pro-football for the Birmingham Mules. We were better known as the Birmingham Jack asses."

"Bubba I bet you could play today. You look in good shape. I bet you lead a clean life and do a lot of jogging."

"Awe, Georgia, I could play today iffin the money was right. The son-of-bitches want you to play for free today. I needed me a vacation anyway. Say I like this song, want to dance before the dance floor gets too crowded?"

Bubba and Georgia were cheek to cheek. Suzie yelled that the music had stopped. Later, after many drinks, Bubba and Georgia were in a passionate embrace when Gator came in and made a bee line for their booth and whispered in Bubba's ear. Bubba jumped up and began cussing Gator. "Keep your filthy mouth shut about this lady … you hear me now, you get the hell away from us before I stomp a mud hole in yore ass and wade it dry."

Gator, with a hurt look on his face, left in a hurry, and Bubba and Georgia went back to smooching. Bubba's hands were like a octopus … clutching and groping all over Georgia. While groping, he suddenly broke off his lip lock on Georgia and backed off with a puzzled look on his face. He let out a yell, jumped up and over-turned the booth. He wrapped his hands around Georgia's throat and her blond wig fell off. With his face red and perspiring, He began to scream at Georgia. "You ain't gonna fool nobody else you … you damn tran … transvestite!"

The police finally arrived and pried Bubba's fingers from Georgia's throat. It took five policemen to subdue Bubba. Soon everything quieted down and the paramedics arrived to patch up George, who was barely breathing.

Bubba had almost crushed his larynx and forever after he would speak with a hoarse whisper. Bubba had to be restrained and transported to the state mental hospital, where he was admitted and underwent extensive treatment. After his release and for the rest of his life he went berserk every time he saw a blond woman.

The moral to this story is: you can't tell what's in a package by looking at its wrapping.

Bubba's Army Career

Woody

The Vietnam war was going full blast and Uncle Sam was looking for a few good men.

Bubba and Gator were at the Lucky Lotto drinking a cool one. Suzie, the barmaid said that Stumpy had received his draft notice. "Boy is he upset, didn't sleep any last night."

Bubba said the government must be crazy. "Hell, Stumpy can't march. He can hardly walk. Now me and Gator are in good shape. The Feds should take us. I should say we would be in shape if we would lay off the booze and wild women. Say Suzie how about me tending bar while Stumpy is being a soldier?"

Suzie said, "Bubba, you and Gator had better read your mail. You all have two boxes full in the storeroom. Don't be drinking my booze either. Most of it is junk mail, but a couple are from the government."

"Come on Gator, we might have won the Publisher Clearing House sweep stakes." "Hell Bubba, they should quit sending us all this junk mail. We ain't got any money."

Bubba and Gator came back from the storeroom with their tails dragging. Gator ordered a double shot for himself and Bubba.

Suzie asked, "What is wrong?" They both tried to answer at once. Suzie yelled and said "one of you shut up, and tell me what is going on?"

Bubba said, "We got our draft notice. We leave the first of May. This will break my poor Mama's heart. I is her only support."

Gator said, "I don't want to hear that crap. You drink up most of your Mama's social security check. Hell, the only time you go home is when you are broke and hungry."

"You two will be going with Stumpy. Maybe you all will stay together for two years."

The first of May arrived. Bubba. Gator and Stumpy caught the Greyhound bus for Fort Web. Bubba had brought a gallon of old McNutt's white lightning. The jug was passed around and the twenty draftees were feeling no pain.

The bus arrived at Fort Web. They were rudely awakened at 3a.m. by a big ugly drill Sargeant. He yelled "You candy asses get up and pee, the world is on fire."

Bubba belched and rubbed his eyes and said, "Gator I think we have died and gone to hell. That big Sargent must be the devil."

The draftees were herded into a gym where the drill Sargent had them to strip down to their birthday suit. The Sargent spread the rumor that they would get a shot in their left testicle with a square needle. Some of the men fainted and were revived by smelling salt.

The men were sent from table to table where their blood pressure and temp was taken. The doctor was located at the last table. He had the final word if you passed the physical.

Bubba stood before the Doc who said, "Bend over and spread your cheeks". Bubba bent over and spread his mouth. The Doc was upset and yelled, "You stupid red neck not them cheeks, I'm checking for hemorrhoids."

The physicals were finally over and the draftees were marched to the clothing warehouse. They were issued one size fits all.

The men thought this night would never end as they were marched to their barracks. The duffle bags felt like they weighed a ton.

They finally reached the barracks and were met by a big Sargent who would be their drill Sargent for the next twelve weeks.

Sargent Mann was his name. He stood six five and weighed two thirty. He was a mean looking S.O.B. Sargent Mann mounted the P. T. stand and yelled, "At ease!" and said, "I will be your Mama and Papa for the next twelve weeks. When I tell you to crap I want you to squat and ask how much and what color. You all follow my orders and we will get along. Cross me and your butt will belong to me."

Next the trials of basic training.

Bubba in Basic Training

Woody

Bubba and Gator spent their first day of basic training trying to avoid the prying eyes of Sargent Mann. Their luck was bad. The Sargent knew their names and knew that they were from the South. He was always bad-mouthing the South. He yelled, "You damn Rebs better shape up! Bubba get Your ass down and give me twenty push-ups! Gator, you and Grady hoist them damn rifles above your heads and give me three laps around the parade ground. Move it! Move it!"

Sargent Mann marched the weary trainees back to their barracks, halted them and said, "When I dismiss this detail, I want you to police the company area and I don't want to see nothing but elbows and assholes. Now, who has the best damn company?"

The men yelled back, "A Company." With a look of scorn, Sargent Mann replied, "Can't hear you ... you bunch of candy-asses." The men yelled back, "A Company!" With a weary sigh, Sargent Mann quietly said, "Dismissed."

After picking up every tiny scrap of trash, Bubba, Gator and Grady staggered into the barracks and were outraged when they saw that their beds were scattered over the barracks floor. Gator said, "Damn ... what'n hell's happened? Some som'bitch gone pay for this. Where's the barracks's ordley? Hey Jake! Jake ... what in hell's this all about?"

Jake said, "Now don't y'all go blamin' me. Sargent Mann done it ... didn't like the way y'all made yore beds ... said theyn weren't tight enough. Boy, was he mad ... said you men spent too much time shooting the shit."

Mumbling threats, they staggered off to the showers. The platoon had divided itself into the North and South. Civil war was being fought all over again. Each side sat together at the mess hall and PX beer garden. The men from the west were left to choose any side they wanted. They did what they could to fuel the flames of controversy between the warring factions.

Bubba, Gator, and Grady were setting over a beer in the planning of how they were going to get even with Sargent Mann. Gator said,

"Let's nail his door shut so's he won't be able to make reveille." Bubba said, "Hell Gator, he'd just break the damn door down and make us fix it back. We need a better plan than that." Grady leaned across the table and said, "How 'bout this?" Mann always goes to the latrine fifteen minutes before wake up call and always uses the same commode. Why don't we get there ahead of him and put some super glue on the toilet seat?"

Bubba grinned and said, "Now, that's one good idee. I can't wait. Let's do it in the mornin'. We'll show that friggin' sargent who's chain he's rattlin'. Gator, you be down there and be ready. When Mann starts down I'll whistle. You fix the toilet seat up and bring the rest of the super glue back up to me. I'm gonna fix me up a couple o' damn Yankees ... make them sons-of-bitches think twice 'fore they mess with us Rebs again."

The next morning their plans went off without a hitch. Bubba had glued the Yanks boots to the barracks floor. While they slept, he had glued their toes and fingers together, glued hands to chest and glued hands to private parts. Sargent Mann clomped down to the latrine and plopped himself down on the toilet seat.

The early morning peace was shattered as all hell broke loose. Sargent Mann was cussing and yelling while trying to get up from the throne. He bellowed, "Somebody's ass going to belong to me when I find the son-of-a-bitch who did this. Hey somebody call the CQ ... get me the hell loose from this commode seat."

Meanwhile the Yanks had been awaken by the sergeant's yelling and cussing. They were going crazy trying to get their hands loose from their body parts. The Rebs were rolling in the barracks floor, laughing. Sargent Mann was screaming holy hell when the CQ arrived.

The CQ took one look at the turmoil and burst out laughing which only served to make Sargent Mann angrier. The CQ called the emergency room, who sent an ambulance.

The ambulance arrived with lights flashing and siren screaming, which drew a crowd at the barracks door. The driver and medic ran into the barracks and found a half-naked sergeant stuck to a toilet seat. Seeing they could do nothing for him they went to the other glue-stuck men and found a similar situation.

24

They put their heads together and conferred a couple of minutes, they called the post engineers.

They arrived and removed the toilet seat from the commode — with Sargent Mann still attached. Amid a lot of whooping and hollering from the onlookers and blistering cussing from the sergeant, they transported sergeant and toilet seat to the hospital emergency room.

While this was going on, the Yanks were becoming desperate. Some had lost bits of skin trying to pry their fingers and toes apart. They were sent to the dispensary. The ones glued to their private parts were sent to the hospital. The doctors on duty at the emergency room had never witnessed a sight such as this. Years later they would burst out laughing every time they thought about the glue epidemic.

After eight weeks the men were getting used to army food and discipline. Bubba, as usual, was bad mouthing the Army. He said, "Them lousy son'bitches are puttin' saltpeter in the coffee. Hell, I ain't got me no kinda sex drive any more. Iffen that ain't enough, they's too many good men gittin' wasted in Vietnam ... papers is full o' horror stories 'bout that place."

"I gotta get out of this man's army ... say, p'fessor...you a educated man. Tell me how to git outta this chicken-shit outfit, without going to jail."

"Well, Bubba, let me see ... hmmm. How about this? You know they discharge homosexuals if they find out, don't you? Why don't you claim to be one and you'll be home before the week is out."

"What if the people at home find out?" "Hell, Walker County is a long way from Fort Jackson. How are they going to find out? When you get home you can tell everybody you've been discharged because of flat feet or bad hearing or something like that."

"You know, I just might do that. Thanks P'fessor...I'll sleep on it and see how I feel tomorr'."

The next morning, while the rest of the platoon was asleep, Bubba got up, went over and sat on the floor between Gator and Grady's bunk and whispered, "Y'all awake?"

"We are now," whispered Gator. "What t'hell we whispering about?" "I'm gonna do it ... I'm going to get me outta this place."

At reveille Bubba went on sick call to put his plan into effect. The medic who screened sick call, called Bubba to his desk and said,

25

"What's your problem, soldier…, got a cold…VD … the clap?" He looked up at the mumbling Bubba and said, "Say, what!"

Bubba was whispering that he was homosexual to the medic, who kept yelling. "Speak up… speak up, dammit! I can't hear you!" This caused Bubba to yell so loud that the whole post soon knew that he was a homosexual.

In a shaking voice, the medic said, "Uh … I don't … uh … you'all have to see the headshrinker." He pointed a shaking finger and said, "Right over there in that corner." Bubba went over to the psychiatrist's desk, stood before him and thought, "Hell, I've gone this far … might as well go all the way."

The psychiatrist tapped his pencil eraser on his desk for a couple of seconds, looked up and said, "Now Boy, let's see … say you don't like women, huh?

Bubba said, "Yes, Sir … I mean'…no sir! I'm a homosexual and I want to go home to be with my lover, who is a pulp-wood cutter back in Alabama."

Gator and Grady had hung around pretending they were policing trash — watching the door to the dispensary, when the door flew off its hinges with a red-faced Bubba right behind it. They watched with open mouths as Bubba, cussing a blue streak, ran back to the barracks as fast as he could get there. They followed him into the barracks, over to his bunk, where he was shaking with uncontrolled wrath. Both talking at once, they wanted to know what happened, when was he going home.

Bubba, almost too angry to speak, sputtered, "Uh … uh … got ambushed by that damn shrink bastard. When I told him I was queer … he … he zipped open his fly an…an' said, 'Prove it, '." "…Damn son'bitch … looks like I'm gonna go to Nam with you guys after all."

Bubba Goes To Nam

Woody

Bubba, Gator, Grady, Professor and Billy Joe were dressed for the graduation parade. Laying around waiting for the whistle to blow for them to fall in, "Bubba said I am glad to get out of this hell hole. I will probably see Sargent Mann in my dreams. I still laugh when I picture Mann and the commode seat being loaded in the meat wagon."

"Grady, are we getting our orders after the parade?" "Yeah. I just hope we aren't going to Nam. I heard the last bunch, went straight to Nam. Some of them have already bought the farm."

Sargent Mann yelled, "Fall in you ass holes. This is my happy day. My last day with you Rebels. Bubba you and your bunch of Rebels act nice for one day. I hope to hell I never see you Rebs again. You all have made my life hell the pass twelve weeks. Some of you men will be going to Nam. I hope you serve your country with pride and honor."

The graduation parade went smoothly. Sally Joe and Suzie were in the stands, yelling and waving. Suzie said, "There goes Bubba. I will be damn he looks in good shape. I don't guess he could drink and whore around like he did when he was home. I am glad that Stumpy went through medical school instead of Infantry training. I don't think Stumpy will go to Nam. His leg is too short and I am pregnant." Sally Joe said, "Me and Bubba will work on me getting pregnant while he is home on two weeks leave. If he stays sober long enough maybe Bubba will ask me to marry."

That Greyhound bus could be heard miles away before arriving at the Lucky Lotto. Amos, the new bartender, was polishing the bar and thinking what Bubba and the rest of the Rednecks would think of a black man tending bar. "Hell, I fought and played football with Bubba when we were with the Birmingham Jackasses. Things shouldn't be to bad."

Amos couldn't believe his eyes; the bus stopped and a whole load of drunk GIs got off. The joint would be rocking tonight. Sally Joe and Suzie were off the bus first, followed by Bubba, Gator Grady,

Billy Joe and the Professor, who decided to spend his leave with his new found friends. They staggered through the front door And Bubba yelled, "If it ain't old Amos. Good to see you, you black SOB. Give us all a big cool one."

Amos served the drinks and said, "These are on the house. Nothing is too good for our fighting men. Bubba you look good.

I bet you in better shape than when you played for the Jack asses."

"You bet Amos. I is one lean mean fighting machine. Me, Gator, Grady, Billy Joe and the Professor are going to Nam to kick asses and take names. We can't write so that only leaves butt kicking. Hey Suzie, when is your old man coming home? I need me a personal medic and pill pusher. I am going to make love not war." Suzie said, "Bubba, you are crazy as a bessie bug. You will be making war not love. Don't do anything stupid or you will come back in a body bag."

Sally Joe was talking to the Professor. "How come you are mixed up with Bubba, Gator, Grady and Billy Joe?" "Well Sally, I like these Rebs. They take care of each other. I figure by sticking with them I stand a better chance of coming back from Nam. I should have some fun also."

What Goes Around, Comes Around

Woody

Sergeant Tay met the bus at the replacement center, called their names, and sent them to draw weapons and field gear. You men will be going to your units tomorrow.

After they had receive their weapons and field gear, they were to go to the hootch to spend the night before going to their unit. As they entered the hootch they heard a familiar voice. "Keep the damn noise down or your ass belongs to me." Bubba started cussing. "I must be having a night mare or better still a mule. Is that you Sergeant Mann? This is a small world. Say its ain't so. Some one wake me up from this night mare."

Sergeant Mann said, "I wish I could say you Rebs were a welcome sight, but this is my worst night mare coming true. Surely they won't send me to the same unit as you shit heads."

Tay called the roll the next morning and Sergeant Mann and the rest of the Rebs were assigned to the 25th Divison - the Wolfhound Regiment. Bubba said, "Mama said I was going to the dogs and now its true."

The truck arrived at the 27th Headquarters. Mann had complained all the way to the unit. The truck was met by a Sergeant in shower shoes who showed them bed. "These beds belonged to men who went home in body bags. Put your equipment away and we will go to the club and drink a few cool ones."

Gator said, "Did you see his feet, Bubba? It must be jungle rot. His toes were about to fall off."

The Rebs walked into the club and heard a familiar voice. Amos was setting with Stumpy complaining about the heat and food. "I should have stayed at the Lucky Lotto. My big mouth got my black ass sent to this hell hole. How did Suzie take it when she found out you were coming to Nam?"

"Well, Amos she did throw a hissey. Said she hopes I don't get in the same outfit that Bubba and his bunch are in. She is going to have a baby and I want to make it home in one piece."

29

Bubba finally walked over to the bar and covered Amos's eyes and said, "guess who... you black bastard." "I don't have to guess. That is you ... Ain't it, Bubba? Its got to be you or I am having a night mare." "Yeah..., It's me you big ass hole. Stumpy, I will be damn. How come you are here? Couldn't stay away from your friends...Huh?"

"Hey, Popa San, bring us a round of drinks. We are going to howl tonite. The old gang is together again. Sergeant Mann came in and said, "You Rebs should take it easy on the booze. We are in a combat zone. I have to go to Battalion. The Battalion Commander wants to see me. Said it was important."

The boys were back in the hootch when Sergeant Mann returned. He didn't look too happy. "The Engineering Commander wants me to make a platoon out of you guys and go on a recon patrol. Bubba, you will be the first squad leader, Amos you will have the second. Professor, you will be my radio operator. The Battalion. is sending two dogs and their handlers over. We fly out on choppers at 3am, so get some sleep."

The dogs arrived. Smitty and James were their handlers. The dogs looked better than their handlers. Smitty spoke up and said don't pet or feed the dogs. Chief is the scout dog's name. Hitler is the attack dog. As you can see Hitler has his fangs capped.

Bubba said, 'You guys have been here twelve months. Aren't you scared when the shooting starts?" "Well ... some people act different. I have seen officers crap in their pants. Some guys freeze, completely crack up. Hell I just think of it as a job."

Mann came by and said, "Knock off the chatter and get some sleep. Three a. m. comes early." The choppers landing woke the platoon. Mann was checking the men's basic loads of ammo and to make sure that their dog tags were taped together. "Bubba, take your squad and load in the first chopper. The dogs will be with you. Amos, you and your squad will be on the last chopper. Stumpy, you will be with Amos. Me and professor will be in the second chopper. Lets load up and go kick some ass."

The choppers were only airborne for about ten minutes when the door gunner signaled that they were at the LZ. The choppers dropped like a rock in the LZ. the men bailed off and set security around the LZ.

Bubba said, "Is that you Amos? I can only see two eyeballs. Damn, I couldn't see a VC if he was two feet in front of me."

"Yeah ... Bubba, its me. I am scared shitless. I ain't never killed any body. I'se cut a few, but they lived to tell about it. Hey ... the dogs have spotted something out front. I had better tell Mann."

Professor's radio crackled. He relayed Amos' message to Mann. Mann said, "Ask how many VC are out there?" Smitty said, "Tell Mann he can come out here and count the VC. We only spot them." The hair on Hitler's back, the attack dog, was standing straight up. He was ready to take a bite out of somebody's butt. The dogs gradually relaxed. The VC were moving away from the platoon. The battalion radioed Sergeant Mann at daylight; he was to check out the village of Cue, Chie. There was supposed to be a regiment of VC there.

Sergeant Mann was cussing and muttering ..."What to hell are we going to do with them when we find them?" The platoon moved out on a jungle trail to the village Cue, Chie. Visibilty was just about zero. The dogs were in front with their handlers. The column stopped;Smitty had signaled that the dogs had spotted a booby trap. Mann asked for a volunteer to disarm the booby trap. No one answered his call, so he had to move forward and disarmed the booby trap.

The platoon moved out and one hour later came in view of the village. Mann halted the platoon and took out his field glasses and carefully scanned the village. The village looked so peaceful that he almost ordered the platoon to go in. As Mann scanned the area again, he got the shock of his life. There was a Battalion of VC coming into the village. The Professor radio the information to Battalion. They said to stay in position and observe and report all movement. Mann passed the word around that no one was to fire on any thing unless he gave the orders.

Red Neck Reunion

Woody

The Lucky lotto's parking lot was full of pickup trucks. They were here for the Redneck reunion. This was a gathering of all mobile Rednecks.

If you knew Redneck culture. You could tell where the trucks came from, by just looking at the bumpers and the trinkets hanging from the mirrors.

The Alabama trucks had coon tails hanging from their radio antennas. Their bumper stickers said this truck is guarded by a Bulldog with aids and he has Hemorrhoids.

The Florida pickups had gun rack in the rear window-With a big dog in the bed of the pickup.

Georgia's pickups had a pair of dice hanging from the rear view mirror. The bumper sticker said they knew what crack was. Photo on sticker of a man with his jeans down.

The Louisiana trucks had baby Gators hanging from their mirrors and a bumper sticker that said 'thank God they weren't from Mississippi.'

The Texas trucks had cow horns and a sticker that said Cow Paddy champion 96.

Arkansas had Pig snouts on their mirrors. No bumper stickers. The trucks didn't have bumpers.

Mississippi had a toy dog on the mirror. Their trucks were without bumpers also.

Bubba and Gator were sitting at the bar drinking a cool one and talking NASCAR. Gator asked Suzie about Bubba,

Suzie said, "Bubba is getting a pass to attend the reunion. Bubba does OK as long as he takes his medication and don't see any blondes. He called and said he was sorry about the ruckus about George. I told him it was partly my fault for introducing him to Georgianna."

"Hey … girls? How are y'all coming on the wet T-shirt contest?" "Gator, this is Velma, Thelma, Sally Joe and Joe." Joe spoke up and said "Don't ya'll get the idea I'm like George. I have the credentials to prove I am one-hundred percent woman. Y'all hang around for the wet T-shirt contest and I will prove it."

Billy Joe said, "Gator did you see them guys selling that Wacky Weed in the parking lot when you came in? Hell there are so many of them that they have to wear arm bands to keep from trying to sell to each other."

"Gator this is going to be some party. The law must be blind. Say did you pick up some shine from Old Mac Nutt?"

"Yea, I got some and it is good stuff. You can see the bead in it. Works good in your Zippo cigarette lighter too."

"Hey, isn't that Bubba in the parking lot? Billy Joe, would you go out and talk to him. I don't want any trouble. I hope he isn't still mad about George."

Billy Joe met Bubba in the parking lot and shook hands. Billy Joe said, "You look well-fed and rested."

"Well, I'll be damn if it ain't ole Billy Joe. You are as ugly as ever. If I had a dog that look like you, I would shave his ass and make him walk backwards."

"Yes sir, the same old Bubba. I want to ask you something personal. You still got a case of hips at Gator?"

'Hell, no, Billy Joe. I have been thinking it over. Gator probably saved me from marrying George. I am slowly getting back to normal. What ever normal is?"

Billy Joe and Bubba walked back to the bar. Bubba came over to Gator and said, "I am sorry about the fight we had over George. Can we be friends again?"

"Hell, Bubba, I have forgotten all about it. Sit down and I will buy you a drink."

When Suzie came over to take their order, Bubba said, "There is a bunch out in the parking lot high on shine and pot. They might start trouble."

"Stumpy is ready for trouble. He has his double barrel shot gun loaded with rock salt and a baseball bat. We just finished redoing this place and we won't stand for any fighting in here. Some of them rednecks will have red heads when I get my pool cue working on their heads."

"Gee, I wish they had nurses in the nut house that looked like you girls. I would volunteer to stay. I can't wait for the contest to start."

Sadie Mae

Woody

I received a call from Sargent Major John Woodley, my baby brother, who was stationed in Germany. His artillery brigade was shipping out for Desert Storm, where they would kick Hussein's butt and be home in a month. He needed someone to take his children or his dog. He gave me a choice: his dog or his heathen kids. I naturally took the dog, a basset hound named Sadie Mae.

Sadie was flying out the next day on Delta Airlines, who were to call and give me her arrival time. They called and said that Sadie Mae would arrive at 8 p.m. Friday. That day, when Elaine and I left for Birmingham, we were filled with great anticipation for the new addition to our family.

When we arrived at the Delta ticket counter, we were informed that Sadie Mae would come into the freight depot. They gave me some papers and I took them around to the freight depot where there was a large crate waiting. The clerk took the papers, stopped at the large crate and, "This is it!" He tried to move the crate and got a hernia for his effort.

I helped him to get the crate onto a cart so we could move it to my car. It felt like the crate was made of steel, but hell, all the weight was inside. Sadie weighed ninety-seven pounds.

Sadie woke up when we got her to the car, at which time she let out a long mournful howl. I would not be surprised if she was heard around the entire air terminal. I opened the crate and Sadie Mae crawled into the back seat of my car. I threw her two large dog biscuits to gnaw on while we traveled to Jasper.

On the trip home we stopped at Bruno's Super Market to get Sadie some dog treats. Elaine went into the store while I waited in the car with Sadie. She crawled up front where she made herself at home in Elaine's seat.

When Elaine arrived back at the car, Sadie refused to move. Elaine rode the rest of the way home in the back seat. I got my first good look at Sadie after we got home. She was a sad looking hound.

Hell, her ears and belly touched the carpet. She was so ugly, she was beautiful. I fell head-over-heels in love with her.

What a mess she made when she ate. When she finished I had to take a shop vac to clean up after her. My friends and neighbors advised me to keep Sadie Mae chained. They said someone would steal her. Hell, I figured if they could lift her they could have her. I decided that chaining her would be like jail, so I let her run loose with my other half breed mutts.

Sadie was under foot at all times. When I was working in the garden; she would lay on my tomato plants and flatten them. How could I get mad when she gave me her sad and woeful look. I couldn't. I just forgave her.

There is a reclaimed strip pit close by where I take my dogs and let them run. One day the dogs and Sadie Mae jumped a rabbit and the chase was on. Sadie brought up the rear with her short legs. When the rabbit did a stop or turn, Sadie bowled over the other dogs. She gave moral support with her howls.

One Christmas the Vietnam Combat Vets were to give the animals at the Humane Society a party. We decided to let Sadie Mae play Santa. I got a Santa's cap for her and cut holes in it for her ears. When I pulled her ears through the holes in the cap, I fell down laughing. Hell, she looked more like a clown than Santa. I made the trip to the Humane Society with Sadie hanging her head out of the window-howling and getting people's attention. I am proud to say she was the star of the Christmas party. Many people wanted to buy or adopt her. Naturally I refused all offers.

Spradlin Hollow Homecoming - 1945

Bart Country

A rickety old Ford pick-up truck rattled and clanked along the deserted gravel country road, stirring up a whirlwind of yellow dust. Its occupants, a hitch-hiking soldier and the driver, had ridden the better part of a mile since either had last spoken when the soldier broke the silence.

"If you don't mind, good buddy, let me out at that ROCK CITY sign up ahead". The truck shuddered to a wheezing stop at the sign, scattering gravel in all directions.

The soldier had his hand on the door latch, ready to get out, when the driver said, "Looks like it's gonna rain any minute. It's just a few miles to town, Sergeant. Come on in with me and I'll treat you to some supper."

The soldier smiled and said, "I 'preciate that now, but it's eleven miles 'round that hill from town to where I live." Pointing off to the right where a weed-choked path zigzagged up to a low smudge of hills, he said, "It's only two miles by that path over the hill to home. I've had me a lot of practice walkin' in the rain and a little more sure ain't gonna hurt me. Anyway, it won't take me long to walk over it."

The driver nodded and said, "Sure. Well, good luck." The soldier opened the door and heaved himself heavily out of the pick-up, leaned on the truck bed and lifted out his duffel bag. He grinned again at the truck driver and said, "Much obliged anyway, buddy," and closed the door.

Scratching gravel, the truck came to life with a grinding of gears, and wrapped in a billowing shroud of dust rattled out of sight.

The soldier, still hearing the pick-up's diminishing clatter, turned to face the barely visible patch and shouldered his duffel bag. His sturdy six-foot frame was dressed in army issue: olive drab wool trousers, cotton khaki shirt, wool olive drab Eisenhower jacket and dusty combat boots. On his left breast he wore a blue and silver combat infantry badge and a double row of colorful campaign ribbons. Under all this he had pinned a discharge pin, jokingly called a ruptured duck.

At the top of his left arm was the red keystone insignia of the Twenty-eighth Infantry Division, cross-stitched above sergeant stripes. Over his right pocket was the Presidential Unit Citation—a blue ribbon surrounded by a gold border.

As he quickly walked up the path, ragweed and blackberry thorns slapped and grabbed at his legs while he silently counted marching cadence— mentally still in the army.

After about fifteen minutes he reached the foot of the ridge where the weeds along the path gave way to hillside scrub and small rock outcroppings. He shifted the duffel to his other shoulder as he neared the top.

Breathing heavily, he came to a mass of huge rugged boulders scattered across the summit, as if by some angry giants. In among the rocks grew a smattering of haw trees, a few post oaks, and here and there some scrawny pine trees. As he rounded the last boulder that obstructed his view of the valley, a small gust of wet wind tugged at his trousers and a few drops of rain pelted his face. He stopped next to a small rock and put his duffel on some withered tufts of grass and sat down on the rock. He removed his wool overseas cap, fingered its blue infantry piping and then looked down on the valley that was partially obscured by mist and drizzle.

What had been his happy valley when he left for the war now looked like a lonesome valley. As his eyes searched through the gloom for familiar landmarks, the overcast began to break and rays of sunshine slanted down in satiny golden shafts illuminating parts of the valley. Cloud shadows rippled over the valley floor like swift rolling ocean waves. There! There along the river he could see the big meadow with the grassy knoll where he and his sweetheart, Millie, lay on their stomachs close to each other in the hot grass one burning August afternoon, holding hands and watching her daddy and the other mowers cut and bale the hay field. And there! There to the left of that he could see the hackberry grove where he and Percy, his best buddy, played Indians so many summers ago, when he wanted the idle days of summer to last forever. Percy is now under a white cross, in an immense field of white crosses, somewhere in Luxemburg.

Although he knew he wouldn't be able to see it, his eyes searched for the place, where one May morning, he lay beside the remains of a picnic lunch, while Millie braided garlands of violets, and laughing at him, hung them around his neck—the perfume of the violets still strong inside his head.

In a silky streak of sunlight he saw the little white clapboard Baptist church with its plain spire—no cross on the steeple because the congregation didn't believe in that sort of embellishment. It was enough for them that the cross was stamped indelibly on their hearts. The sight of the church and the tombstones behind it roused him from his reverie.

He pushed himself up from the rock, grunted and stretched, lifted his duffel and proceeded down the hill toward a road that would pass by the church. Amid the shirring and clicking of autumn insects he forded a nearly dry brook, crossed a no-longer cultivated field overgrown with weeds and goldenrods in full bloom to where the path entered the road. Here he paused to stare at a run-down half fallen-in cabin that was once a beer joint everybody derisively called "Squeeze Inn" because it was only a one small slab-sided room. Shaking his head, he walked on to the churchyard. He stopped and gazed at the freshly painted church. Right there behind that corner was where Millie first let him kiss her, the summer when they were both fifteen—the summer during that revival meeting when Old Man Tatum and his two sons got salvation amid joyful jubilation.

Having had enough 'remembrance of things past' he smiled ruefully and mumbled, "I gotta stop here and talk to Mama before I go on home."

As he slowly walked the path around the church to where the graves were, he was now limping slightly from a shrapnel wound he had taken liberating a shell-blasted little town in Belgium. The rain clouds had scudded off to the northeast and the sun was hanging low in the west. A strong amber light suffused the air and reflected saffron yellow off the grave stones. The yellow melted to a hot Vermillion. As he looked at the newest grave in his family's plot the sun sunk into a blood red haze and just before it disappeared completely, there came from the back of the cemetery the raucous cawing of crows coming to roost.

He stepped toward the grave. A small breeze stirred and scuffed and scratched through the crisp dead leaves of the harvested cornfield bordering one side of the cemetery. A small night creature skittered away through some fallen leaves between the graves.

The full and heavy rufous harvest moon of October strained up from the horizon. Sharp cold does not arrive here in October, but a comfortable snap was in the air that flowed down from the hills to tell him that the stinging frosts were not far away.

He dropped his duffel bag on a square grave stone next to his Mama's grave, sat on it, lowered his head and said in a quiet voice, "Hello, Mama. This is Ollie. I just got home. I couldn't come home for the funeral—you know I couldn't. The Red Cross got word to me but I couldn't come anyway. War doesn't work like that."

"You know, Mama, the worst thing about being way off in a war is not really knowin' what's goin' on back home. Duty, dirt, death all around you—you kinda get use to that. What you never get use to is the wonderin, and worryin' if there's trouble back home and they might need you there. It gnaws at you all the time."

He stopped talking and gazed blankly at the grave, as if waiting for an answer, then very softly said,

"Mama, I've been through so much a man should never have to go through. I can't even cry anymore. I don't have any tears left in me. There's a long string of my tears from Normandy to Germany and a lot of my tears are in Luxemburg where Percy is buried; but most are in Belgium where I was when the Red Cross told me you had died. I don't think I'll ever be able to cry again."

In the silence that followed he knew he was really home when he heard the sounds of early evening, the same familiar sounds that he yearned for when he was far away in the war the melancholy sing-song of cicadas, the mournful voice of a howling hound treeing a possum somewhere in the hills and the long wail of a freight train approaching a crossing far down the valley. Off somewhere there was the sharp flat slap of a slammed screen door and the gleeful calling of children, muffled by distance, sounding like a flock of sparrows. Then there was quiet and he was left alone in the gathering darkness.

Hanging his head, he scuffed the ground with the toe of a boot, looked again at the grave and said, "Mama, you remember how Millie and me planned to get married when I got out of the army? Well, I'm out of the army but I don't much think we will now."

"Aunt Louise wrote and told me about every little thing that went on 'round here and a lot of things that probably didn't."

"You know Aunt Louise. She said that after your funeral Millie would come over every day to comfort Papa. She must have done a good job of comforting 'cause Aunt Louise said that Millie is expectin' a baby now."

"I can't help thinkin', like I told you, that if I'd been here at the time, things might have turned out different. Now, I don't know what I'm gonna do. I've got to work it all out some way. First I'll have to go see Papa; I'll have to go see Millie; I'll have to go see Aunt Louise; I'll sure have to go see Percy's Mama and Daddy. After that, maybe I can start puttin' my mind together."

"You know, Mama, it's kinda funny. I know how to face a German panzer division but I don't know how I'm gonna face all this."

From high above and out of sight came the haunting cries of a flight of geese, winging south to their winter lakes and marshes; their honks fading to muted chuckles as they sailed past the rising moon and over the hills. He looked up as if he might see them, then turned to the grave again. He unbuttoned his jacket pocket and took out a paper flower, a red Flander's poppy, he had picked up somewhere in France and kept with him. It was crumpled and flattened but the crape paper petals were still bright red.

He stooped over and carefully placed it on the grave. In a voice of hushed sorrow he said, "Well I gotta go now. Goodnight, Mama. Pray for me."

The Ballerina

Ramonia Evans

In 1977, 1 became a 'Damn Yankee'! I earned this questionable honor by marrying a Southern Gentleman and moving us, furniture, dog, young-uns, accents and all from Iowa to Alabama to live.

My husband, Jim, who actually describes himself as a "Hillbilly, an educated Hillbilly," was quick to inform me that a Yankee is one who comes to stay! And I did mean to stay.

My sons, who had been born and raised in Los Angeles, California, looked around Oakman, Alabama, population 300, with glazed eyes. Scott, who was 15 years old, announced that he thought I had brought them to the end of the world. All three of them informed me daily that as soon as they turned 18 they were moving back to California! I told them that was fine. They are all now in their early thirties. All three married southern girls and none of them live in California.

They began adjusting as soon as they started school here. They were accepted and popular with the boys because all three played sports and the girls thought the "new boys" were so cute with their "northern brogue" and their California origins. We lived in a little rented house in Oakman for one year while our new house on the farm was being built. We lived right across the street from the car wash and next to the "washer." I think Oakman must have had the cleanest young girls that year. Every time I looked up, there were groups of them washing cars or clothes, waving and calling out to the boys.

I actually think Tim, Scott, and Kevin had an easier adjustment than I did. It seemed whenever I spoke to someone, after about three sentences they would look at me with a puzzled expression and ask, "Say what?" "You're not from here, are you?' Sometimes this was offered with a disdainful look and sometimes with an interested expression. I must admit that I didn't always understand my new southern neighbors either. This included my husband. I didn't know if he wanted some tape or a drink or what when he asked me to scotch his wheels.

I hadn't a clue when he asked me to bring his "toos," (tools). Nor did I when he asked me the whereabouts of his flyer (flare) so he could make a list. I learned that all plants are "flowers" whether or not they have blooms. I learned about high sheriffs and decorations and fa-so-la singing and all day singing with dinner on the grounds. I saw my first quilting frames. I learned how to make "homebrew" for my husband in a big crockery jug, which I learned was a "churn." I learned that what I had always known as a stocking cap was a "boggin." I also learned that most things have two names. I was "that Yankee woman" who married James Arley. There was sweet-milk, truck-wagon, church-house, and home-place.

I learned about being 'carried" places and about "you-all." I had always said "you-guys." The error in my speech was immediately pointed out to me: in that part of the group I was speaking with were in fact "gals" and not guys at all! So, therefore, you-all was much more appropriate. They had a point!

Also, I learned that rather than being an excellent cook I had been considered in Iowa and California, I was really rather pitiful, and in the area of fixing homemade from-scratch biscuits and cornbread every single day, I was actually sorry! My corned beef and cabbage, my Mexican food, Italian food and casseroles were definitely looked on with suspicion. Even my husband, who had lived many other places as he had been in the Navy for many years, would often poke his dinner warily with his fork and ask, "What's this?" I was introduced to okra, grits, red-gravy, poke salad, buttermilk, sweet potato pie, red velvet cake and banana sandwiches, none of which I had ever tasted, nor in most cases ever heard of.

All of this made me realize that I had to make this second marriage work! I had already learned to cook two entirely different ways for different husbands, and God knows what a third would be wanting to eat! I knew I surely didn't want to find out! Everyone was nice and friendly to me and many older women tried to take me under their wing.

Our closest neighbor, Miss Myrt, wanted to teach me to fire a pistol, and cautioned me to carry one with me at all times. My Mother-in-law pointed out to me what pretty glasses Bruton snuff came in, and advised me that if I took up the habit, I could have a whole set in no time. I declined both offers. My sister-in-law thought

I was a little slow because I didn't want to trade my nice car for a pick-up truck.

Her husband could not understand why I took the Birmingham News as he said he knew for a fact that I didn't know a soul over there. As soon as we started building our house, I found that the difference in Jim's dream house and mine was "interesting," but we compromised. I had to. (Remember the cooking?) Finally it was ready and we moved in. It was so nice. My sons and I had never lived in the country before, so this took some getting used to: The well for water, the distance to town, and the quiet.

Soon Jim got the bright idea to raise hogs. It sounded fairly simple to me. They're in a pen, you feed them, they get big, you haul them off to be butchered and behold, pork-chops, ham, etc. It was fine at first, just like I anticipated. About six months into my new career as hog-lady, Jim brought home six more half grown hogs.

One of them was a runt, much smaller than the rest with what looked liked a cleft palate. She was not a pretty animal, but she was talented. She would get a running start and jump over any fence, high, low, electric—any fence!! In mid air she was so graceful, with her legs poised just so. So we named her the Ballerina and watched her leaps with amusement. Until one day she began to organize her fellow hogs. They had all been watching her and learned to jump the fence also. You never saw such a sight as all those fat, ugly hogs leaping all those fences. But it was not amusing long. They got in our garden. They got up on Mother's porch and ate all her dogs' food. They ran away and got in the neighbors' yards and gardens. WHAT A MESS!

Jim was at work on the railroad in the daytime, and the boys were at school, so it fell to me to round up the hogs and drive them home. I put grease on cornbread and crumbled it up to make a trail so they would follow me back in. Unless a car came by, in which case they would scatter and I'd have to start all over. I had to figure out wonderful things to feed the Ballerina so she'd be happy in the pen and not escape, This was not one of the high points of my life.

I was relieved when Jim announced that it was cold enough now that he and some of the neighbor men were going to butcher on Saturday, so Miss Graceful was at the top of the list. I had never heard Jim mention any experience in butchering, but I didn't ask any questions.

Our house sits atop a hill and the "men-folks" set up their butchering operation down in the pasture at the foot of the hill. Needless to say I stayed in the house on top of the hill.

I don't know if Jim and the others used standard procedures, since this was our one and only experience killing hogs. I gathered from later conversation that first they shot them, then hung them from a tree to cut their throats, then poured boiling water over them. Then they threw the carcasses on my picnic table and cut them in pieces, breaking my picnic table to pieces in the process. The next step was to put the meat in a #3 washtub and bring it up to me.

I was in the kitchen with my kettles for rendering lard and my freezer paper and tape and baggies and such, thinking I was ready, but believe me I was not. I took one look at that big tub of warm bloody chunks of meat and I did not recognize one single cut. It was all cut up some old fashioned way with what I later learned was a big strip of tenderloin instead of pork-chops, etc. I sat down and just looked at it and cried. I felt like Claudette Colbert in that movie I had seen so long ago, "The Egg and I." But you can't keep a good woman down, so I got up and washed the meat and just packaged it in blobs that looked like the right size for one meal and taped it and put it in the freezer. I put the fat I had painstakingly trimmed from the meat in a big kettle and rendered it down for lard and cracklings. When that process was done, I poured it in my clean white plastic containers. You guessed it!! They weren't made from the kind of plastic that lard comes in from the store, and it all melted all over my stove, cabinets, floor, EVERYTHING! What a mess. This time I really squalled! The Ballerina had triumphed.

After this fiasco, we drove the hogs live to Thatch where they were butchered, and pork chops and all the rest was frozen.

When our remaining hogs were finally gone, we got out of the hog business. I think Jim was as disillusioned with his end of the deal as I was mine, since he has never again mentioned raising hogs. The meat was delicious but I can never took at pork in quite (or ballerinas) the same way.

My Southern education continues, as now even after 18 years. I still learn more about it all the time.

Philip and Clothilde

Bart Country

His swarthy face pale and drawn, Jean Philip du Plessis walked slowly through the crowd of fur trappers who were gathered to sell their skins at a rundown warehouse on a bayou near Baton Rouge. With a machete in his left hand and a big black bull whip coiled in his right, he said nothing as he oozed up to each man in the group and stared at him through slitted eyes.

After confronting every man, he turned around, faced them and hissed through clinched teeth, "Some son o' bitch done stole my mushrat skins. I did'n come hundred mile to leave here wit nuttin'. You betta' be hear me now. When I fin' who got my fur he gon' be dead. Nobody be 'bout steal my fur and git away wit it." His ears began to turn red and fire flashed from his beady eyes. "I don' tell you no mo'. I go down to sto' an' when I gits back I betta' fin' my fur in my picks-up truck. You hyeah?"

As he stomped off he uncoiled his whip, flicked it out with a loud crack and took the head off a small green lizard at the edge of the trail. After about twenty minutes he returned, and looking at no one he went directly to his truck. His furs were stacked neatly in a pile in the truck bed. After a quick inventory he saw that not only were all his furs returned, but he had also gained an additional bundle.

After several trips from his truck to where the fur agent was buying the pelts, Jean Philip had built a stack of plews on the table. He got top price because he brought nothing but A-1 quality skins to the sale. After the agent counted out a stack of new twenty dollar bills, Jean Philip rolled them up, slipped them into an empty Bull Durham tobacco sack and stuffed it into his right front pants pocket. Now was the time for some fun. Licking his lips in anticipation, he hurried to the phone booth outside the warehouse and dialed a woman he always stayed with when he was in Baton Rouge.

There were a couple of rings before he heard a click and Clothilde's musical voice came over the phone, "Hello",

"Allo, Clo, this Philip. I just sell my fur and I wan, to see you. You gon' be home?"

Sweetly she crooned, "Oh, Philip, I'm so glad you called. I'm dying to see you. Come on over."

The next four weeks floated by on waves of pleasure. Clothilde was an angel. Nothing was too good for Philip. She willingly, unselfishly satisfied his every desire. When the fur money was spent Philip packed up to go home. A weeping Clothilde begged him to stay longer but Philip said, "I gotta git back to my place. I been gone too long now. Don' you cry, yeh. I gon' come back pretty damn soon, mon petite enfant."

Jean Philip's cabin was ten miles deep in the upper reaches of Lake Bistineau and could be reached only by boat. He kept his truck locked in a shed near the cross-road and poled himself in a pirogue around the swamp. He lived off catfish, crawfish, rabbits, squirrels, wild ducks and a few vegetables he grew in his back yard—mostly okra, pea hot peppers.

One day, several weeks after his return from Baton Rouge, he heard his dogs in a barking frenzy and a long call coming from down the bayou, "'Alooooo, Philip, It's me, Andrew. I'm coming on up there. Don't let dem damn dogs git me."

"Come on up, Handrew. They don' bite nobody. They too lazy. I'm gonna trow 'em to the gators one dese day. What you need?"

"Nothin' now, Philip. I gotta git-, back. You got a phone call from Baton Rouge. Mr. Bailey at the sto' say you gotta call Operator Twenty down there."

"Hokay, Handrew. T'ank you. I be right down.,"

After about an hour of poling, Philip pulled up to the store's rickety cypress boat dock. He went directly to the telephone booth and called the Baton Rouge operator. She made the connection and after a few clicks he heard Clothilde come on the phone and the operator said, "Your call to Mr. du Plessis is ready."

Clothilde started to cry. Philip said, "Whatsa matta wit' you, woman?"

Through choking sobs she blubbered, "Oh, Philip, I… I'm ruined. (more sobs) I haven't been sick in two months."

Philip said, "Hell, you locky. We all got de flu up heah."

Big Bucks

Betty Gallman

It paid all right, but I was beginning to smell like a chicken, so I switched to something different in the job line. I went to another department and signed up for Nuclear Physics. The admissions committee told me I would not enjoy the field. They suggested I try computers.

I succeeded. How? I remember what Ben Franklin said, "A Penny saved is a penny earned." I worked hard and saved all my money. After twenty years of working my rear off for other folks I discovered that my assets in the bank, after this long period, amounted to the sum total of $42.50.

I closed out my account at the bank. Later I went to the race track and put every dime of that money on the sickest horse I could find. Odds were 1, 475 to 1. The care takers could not find the oats to feed the critter, so they fed this filly pork and beans and an after dinner cigar.

It was race time! Flosh out of the starting gate, Snow White stumbled over a banana peel, and let out one big aromatic blast (FART). The other' horses, sniffing distress, facing 90 mile an hour headwinds, stampeded over the fence in the opposite direction (even the jockey). Snow White paid off at $62, 000.

I opened up a computer school. Taught Word Perfect and Office 2000. All the students passed. Why? All the words were small and so were the sentences. Any kid could understand it. If the word did not have instant teach, out with it.

If the students had to think, forget it. There had to be instant, if not total, absorption into the students brain.

This is like a fairy tale soon to be made into a movie.

Caddy

Betty Gallman

I look into her eyes, and I wish I could know what her other lives were like before she came into my life. I am most certain it wasn't exactly idyllic. About sixteen years ago, my beautiful calico, Caddy, was a filthy, emaciated cat stalking rats, birds and whatever else she could find at the local cemetery to survive.

My cousin had been at the cemetery doing some work on family graves one morning when she spotted the cat. She had some bread in the trunk of her car. She got it and left it for the cat. She went back several days later to check the graves and the cat -was still there. This time she had some cat food with her. She opened several cans and left it for the cat.

When my cousin left the cemetery she came out to our house.

I over heard her telling my Mom about the cat. My cousin knew she had come to the right place to tell her story. She knew I had a soft spot in my heart for God's critters.

When my son came in from school, I told him the story. He and I got a box and some food, got in my El Camino, and headed for the cemetery. When I had parked and we had gotten out of the truck we started to look for the cat. Sure enough there she was looking at us from behind an old cedar bush.

I called to her and she came out from behind the tree. I would go toward her and she would go backward. I would go backward and she would go forward. This went on for awhile. I started to laugh, my son laughed, but the cat looked at us as if we were idiots.

I went back to the truck and got some food. I held out a can and she slowly came over, but would not get too close. I kept talking to her and finally she let me pet her while she ate. I rubbed her head and talked very softly to her. When she finished eating I picked her up. My son took her and he was giving her gentle strokes.

We took her to the truck and we were about to get in when she darted out the window before I could blink an eye. That cat cut a trail back to that cedar bush so fast that my eyes could not keep up with her. I knew she was trying to tell us something. She would go into the

bushes and out again. I went over to the cedar bush and started to part
the climbs out of the way so I could see. And to my surprise I found
the reason why she would not leave. There in the brush lay a solid
black kitten. I got the little kitten and took it to the truck. The cat was
right with me. She jumped into the truck, and all the time watching to
see where I placed the kitten. I put that black ball of fur into the box.
Mamma cat sat next to me and rode home with us in the truck as if
she had been doing that all her life.

After she spent the night in the bathroom with her kitten, we were
off to the vet's office, where I learned that my new cat and kitten were
in good health despite their previous living conditions. The vet didn't
know how old the cat was but did give a guess of about three to five
years. The kitten was about four weeks old. We headed home.

Next, I pondered what to call her. She was very independent. She
dragged the kitten around with her everywhere she went. In a way she
reminded me of a golfer the way she would pull the kitten down the
hall. Also, she would follow along behind us as we were walking. I
decided to call her CADDY. The kitten, I named him SINBAD, after
the sailor man.

So Caddy too, up residence with us; she stayed at Mom's house
because I had two cats at my place. Mom already had one. Now we
had a total of five cats.

Caddy was street smart, but she liked to play and romp with her
kitten and Mom's cat, P.K. Caddy kept everyone busy seeing that she
had plenty to eat and also some play time with the adults. She rules
the roost around the house.

However, one shadow of a former life remains. When someone
walks through the house she always walks with them, and if that
someone heads for the kitchen Caddy is ahead of them waiting for her
food. But in her present life with Mom and all of us here, Caddy has
nothing to worry about. The cat that seems to need a great deal of
affection gets all the tender loving care she wants. She always greets
you with a certain little low tone meow and a glitter in her green eyes.
That's my CADDY.

Milo

Woody

I hear Milo barking his fool head off. He has the neighbor's cat treed again.

Milo came into the family by chance. My brother, the general, was dating Mary who had bought Milo for her two boys. Milo was to be a house dog. Milo soon outgrew the house. Mary came home from work and Milo was laying on the carpet with what was left of the VCR and telephone. That was the last straw. Milo had to go.

Who else but my little brother would think of but Perry and Elaine's home for homeless critters. Johnny called and gave Milo a glowing report. Said he had papers. I made the remark that my critters had the Mountain Eagle and Birmingham News. Elaine said one more dog wouldn't run our dog food bill up.

Milo was supposed to arrive on the week end. Johnny called and said he was having trouble getting a cage for Milo to ride in. He didn't tell me he had to have a extra large one.

Monday morning I heard my little critters yelping their fool heads off and a loud roar. I looked out in the driveway and saw John's truck with a big head looming above the cab, roaring its fool head off. Milo was home. We unloaded the big horse and he started planting wet kisses all over me.

I couldn't believe it when Mary said he was only eight months old. Just a baby as she put it. My other two outside dogs are part Great Danes and Labs. Satellite and Bigfoot are big dogs but they look like midgets beside Milo.

Milo's first week was a doozey. Every morning was an adventure. The lawn would have the neighbors toys scattered everywhere. I would find basketballs, footballs and even a small bicycle. The kids now keep their toys put away. Since Milo can't get toys he brings home logs.

When Milo turned eleven months, it was time for his visit to the Vet. I was counting on having trouble getting him into the car and the Vet's office.

Milo crawled in the car like he owned it and made himself at home. When we arrived at the Vet's we caused a small riot. Milo went into the Vets office like he owned it. Of course he tried to slobber on everyone. Milo tipped the scales at 195 pounds.

Milo has changed the scenery here on the hill. People driving by will stop and stare and drive off muttering to themselves.

My Pretty Frauleins

Woody

April, 1955. I had been ordered overseas again—Germany this time—and was home on furlough before I was to report.

While I was enjoying my leave, I became engaged to my current sweetheart, a local girl. My father, mother and her family thought we would get married before I left Germany, but I put it off because I had decided that I had more wild oats to sow.

At the bus station, when my leave was over, I again promised my true love, faithfully, that we would get married as soon as I got home from Europe.

When I arrived in Germany, I was sent to a replacement camp outside Stuttgart to await re-assignment. My replacement company was quartered next to a camp of displaced persons, (DP's), who came from areas that were occupied by the Russians.

World War II had ended only ten years before. The displaced women out-numbered their men ten-to-one, because most of the men had been killed during the war. They lived upstairs in unheated buildings, where the bottom floor was occupied by cows, horses, chickens and other livestock. Food was still in short supply. Soap, cigarettes and whiskey brought welcomed money on the black market. We sent our clothes to them to be laundered and they were happy to get the extra money for washing and ironing.

Right away, I had become involved in some crap-games and won fourteen-hundred dollars that was about to burn a hole in my pocket. I asked for a pass so I could check out the local wild life. When I made my plans known, there were plenty of volunteers who were eager to show me the town. I chose Sgt. James, who seemed to know the area, to show me the location of all the houses of ill repute. We picked up our passes and headed for the gate.

There we were mobbed by cab drivers who were clamoring to take us to town. We chose a cab belonging to a little man named Hermann, who could speak some English. As we were getting into the taxi, I suggested to Sgt. James that we should hit a few bars and check out the women. He said "That's what we're here for."

52

I waved some green-backs in Hermann's face and we were off to the Flesh Pots.

I had been under the impression that Sgt. James could speak enough German to get along, but I soon found out he knew only a few cuss words and obscenities. With a combination of bad English, worse German and very good sign language, he gave instructions to Hermann, who understood perfectly what we had in mind.

We soon arrived at a house and were ushered into a big sitting room where drinks were being served by scantily dressed women. Without preliminaries Sgt. James left with one of the girls.

I sat down at a table where I was soon joined by a good-looking blond fraulein. She could speak some English and told me her name was Brunhilde. I ordered drinks for us and we drank while she told me more about herself—that she had fled East Germany ahead of the Russians and was one of the DP's here. About this time James returned with a wide satisfied grin on his face and told me to get off my ass and sample the merchandise. Before I could move Hermann returned to pick us up. I whispered to Brunhilde that I would come back later that night, and we left to paint some more of the town.

We visited all of Sgt. James' favorite bars and after too much Schnapps we were drunk. At one of the last bars that we visited I announced that it was time to return to Brunhilde.

When we walked in I saw her leaning on the bar, waiting for another customer. She saw me come in and hurried to meet me. She took me by the arm and helped me stumble to a back table, where we were joined by Sgt. James and his girl. We had some drinks, and Brunhilde invited me to spend the night with her. Before I accepted, I asked about the price of an all-nighter. She chucked me under my chin, smiled and said, "For you, mein liebling, my love is free."

I laughed to myself "Free my Ass! I've been paying a hell-of-a-steep price for the tea you've been drinking that was supposed to be whiskey."

Hermann was still waiting for us and Sgt. James, his girl, Brunhilde and I left for Brunhilde's room, a cheap hotel at the DP camp.

As we were getting out of the taxi, Brunhilde told Hermann to return the next morning at 9:00 a.m. When I pulled out my wad of money to pay him her eyes almost popped out of her head.

We went inside and by this time Brunhilde was looking really good to me. All four of us got in the same bed and I was so drunk that I have no recollection of what happened after that. When I awoke the next morning, I was afraid to open my eyes because my face was buried in a mass of smelly hair. Boy, was I relieved when I got the nerve to open my eyes and saw it was only Brunhilde's arm-pit. She awakened, got up and fixed us a drink. I felt sure I had lost my roll of money, but to my surprise, she handed me my pants along with all my belongings—including the money.

Brunhilde then invited Sgt. James and his fraulein to eat with us, called room service for some food and the four of us sat down to breakfast in our birthday suits. For those who have a weak stomach, I don't recommend this practice.

We were just finishing when we heard Hermann tooting the taxi's horn, letting us know that it was time to dress and head back to camp.

Before I left the hotel, Brunhilde made me promise to let her know where I was to be stationed when I got my new orders. She said, "Liebling, I will come where you are to keep you company."

Before I was transferred I got to spend three glorious weeks with her. Man, I tell you; I was beginning to like this European culture.

My new orders were cut and I was assigned to the First Missile Command on the other side of Stuttgart. When I reported for duty they didn't have a job for me so the First Sergeant told me that I was the new reveille sergeant. All I had to do was come in at 6:00 a.m. and hold morning roll call; then I was finished for the day.

Sgt. Pierce, the manager of the Non-commissioned Officer's Club, took me under his wing and showed me the best watering holes in town. After visiting a bunch of bars I chose Peggy's Place, because I could see that she ran the best bar in town.

Peggy was in her thirties, red-haired, and built like a brick outhouse. Every time I came into her bar she would playfully check my I.D., tease me about being too young to shave and accuse me of being a virgin.

One day I mentioned to Peggy that I was hunting an apartment, and she said that she had an extra room and offered to rent it to me. I agreed and the first night after I had moved in I brought a woman to my room.

That's when the crap hit the fan. Peggy was furious. She stomped up to my room and raised such holy hell that my fraulein left in a hurry—mach schnell! Peggy then told me, in a way that left no doubt, that she was the only female allowed in my apartment. This was the beginning of my schooling in love making—by a first-class mistress of love. Aphrodite, herself, would have been envious.

Emergency Room

Woody

The emergency room at old Peoples hospital was more like a three ring circus, than a medical facility. These are some of the funniest cases that I saw while working there.

I started working at Peoples hospital in 1971. I expected the hospital to have all the latest medical equipment. I was shocked when I came on duty my first day. Most of the equipment was World War Two vintage. The Nurses and orderlies had a starring role in, "One flew over the Coo Coo nest."

My first day on the job a man came in with wound in the groin. The nurse refused to treat him. Her excuse was that she would have to expose his penis. My question was "how in hell did she become a nurse?"

They did things backwards from the Army. No equipment was checked to see if it was operational. This caused many mishaps, some comical, some serious. The call came down for a code blue. I grabbed the shock cart and headed for the room where code blue was called. After I got to the room, the Doctor and I were the only ones that answered code blue. The doctor was cussing a blue streak, things only got worse. The plug was missing on the crash cart. By some miracle the patient lived. I could find no one in the hospital who was responsible for the maintenance or stocking the cart. Every one passed the buck. Since I raised so much hell they put me in charge of the Emergency Room crash cart.

On one of the episodes I rushed to the patient's room. The doctor was ready to shock the patient. A nurse's hands got in the way. Now we had two patients in cardiac arrest.

The drunks gave the emergency room personnel the most trouble. My job was to soothe the drunk's anger. If the emergency Doc was mad he would suture the wound without Novocain. The place some times resembled Saturday Night wrestling. We got some big mean drunks.

Security was a laugh. The Security guard was either a cousin or uncle of one of the county commissioners. When trouble came in the front door, Security usually left by the back door. Plus most of the security officers were old and on Social Security. Security was what you could provide yourself.

One of the craziest or stupidest stunts I witnessed was the time an orderly rolled a dead man to his room and yelled for him to get out of the chair and get into bed. The dead man fell out of the chair when the orderly touched him.

One night a man came in with a bullet wound to his butt. While the patient was at x-ray the jealous husband came and started firing his pistol down the hallway at the patient. Security was no where to be found. I thought I was back in Vietnam. Some one called the Jasper Police and they said the hospital was private property and their hands were tied. The shooter ran out of ammo and left to get more. The police finally arrested him. I had to drink a fifth after my shift to settle my nerves.

One night a Black Vietnam vet came in overdosed on heroin. He was raising hell. During the scuffle to keep him on the treatment table his ear fell off. The ER nurse fainted thinking that I had cut his ear off. The man was wearing a prosthesis. Hell, most of his face was fake.

Then there was the fish hook caper. The Black lady had been to the Walker County Lake fishing and she had caught a big one. The lady brought the fishing rod with her. She wanted the doctor to come out to the car and remove the hook. She said she was too embarrassed to come into the Emergency room. I finally talked her into coming in for treatment. The doctor sent me to maintenance to get wire cutters. After delivering the cutters I had to leave and confront a drunk, so I missed the delicate surgery. The doctor cracked up when he said she had caught a big black Bass in the lips.

The Emergency Room is the heart of a hospital. It has to operate at a one hundred percent efficiency to save lives and serve the community. This emergency resembled the Hollywood set of the Three Stogies.

Christmas Tree in Hoopla

Woody

Year 1996:

Decorating the Christmas tree had become a chore instead of a pleasure. So this year she just wrapped it in plastic, and put it away in the barn fully decorated, so the next year she wouldn't have that problem.

Year 2095:

The space ship and crew zoomed in on planet Earth. The crew sat in the galley, drinking tea and talking about life they expected to find on planet Earth.

The space ship was from the galaxy Japa, thousands of light years away from the planet Earth. They were dispatched by their supreme Commander to try and save some of the Earth people. To restock the national zoo.

The space ship was traveling at warp speed lO. The ships crew on the Megatron aimed on the death comet heading for planet Earth. The word was radioed to the ship commander that the space was in position to fire on the death comet, but another 24 hours would put the ship in position to do maximum damage to the death comet.

The Megatron was brought up to full charge and zeroed in on the death comet. The Commander hoped to fire the Megatron and move the comet out of the path of Earth and avoid a head on collision with earth. There would be damage to the Earth Atmosphere, some of the oxygen would be depleted, but life would remain on Earth.

Meanwhile on Earth things were moving at a frantic pace. The White House and Congress had left D.C. for the Rocky mountains, where they had and underground city. There was no night time. The Earth was bathed by a thousand suns, and the temperature was rising. The preachers were yelling for all Earthlings to repent.

The Megatron was brought up to full power and zapped at the comet. The shot was a sucess. The Atom wave was dead center, and the Defiant scope spotted the movement of the death Comet away from Earth. The Earth had been saved. The shock wave and gas given off by the death comet, had made time stand still on Earth. If an Earthling diving into a pool, he would be frozen in mid-air. The Earthlings were frozen in some hell of positions and poses.

The space ship landed in Oakman, Alabama behind a barn on this farm. The first vistor out of the space ship stepped in a cow pie. He was glad they didn't have that odor on Hoopla. The Hooplas had no idea what Earth people looked like. The one who stepped in the Cow shit, thought he had stepped on a baby Earthling.

The squad of Hooplas in the barn let out a yell. They had found the King of the Earth with all his jewelry. The space ship Commander ordered the squad to bring the Earth King into the space ship. The Commander decided that the cow dung was food for the Earth King. He ordered that all the empty space be filled with food for the Earth King.

The food was loaded and the King secured in the space ship and the ship was prepared for take off. The Scientist on board set about trying to decipher the English on the King. They figured Merry Christmas was the Kings name.

Baby Factory

Woody

How in hell did I get assigned to the obstetrics ward at Fort Leonard, Missouri, better known as the Baby Factory.

I figured that I was being punished for the jump on Desert Strike. My antics had teed off the Surgeon General of the Army.

While my unit was on Desert Strike, things were slow at the hospital. We were sitting around playing poker and bored to death. I had won all the money and we were playing for match sticks. The booze flowed freely. We got the idea of making a free fall over the volley ball court while the nurses were playing. The Otter pilot assigned to the hospital, in his drunken haze, went along with the deal. The pilot was as crazy as a bessie bug.

Lieutatant Fogarty, the pilot, and I left in the Colonel's jeep for the airfield. We also took along a ample supply of bug juice. The bug juice was made up of two parts 190 proof alcohol and two parts orange juice. It was quite potent.

We made our plans while riding to the airfield. We decided that on the first flyover we would throw out duffle bags to get the nurses' attention. On the second pass Fogerty and I would hit the silk.

After we were finally airborne I told Fogerty that we would have to jump for the pilot was too drunk to land the plane. The 190 was passed around to keep up our courage. The pilot came over the intercom and said to get ready to release the duffle bags. The plane swooped low over the volley ball court and we kicked the bags out. The bags got their attention for they hit a staff car.

The plane gained altitude for Fogerty and me to jump. As I wobbled to the door I yelled for Fogerty to follow me.

I jumped at ten thousand feet. I expected Lt. Fcgerty to follow. It was so peaceful floating down with the air rushing by. I even wished I had brought the jug along.

At fifteen hundred feet I popped my chute and zeroed in on the volley ball court. I could see the nurses waving. Actually they were signaling for me to land as far away from them as I could.

In my drunken daze I thought they were cheering me on. The desert floor came up and met my ascent. I hit pretty hard.

As I collapsed my chute I looked up into the face of an angry three star general. He yelled, "What the hell are you doing? Boy, you had better sell the outhouse for your butt belongs to me." The general put me in for a general court-martial. I thought to myself "there goes my army career". I made it through the summer on Desert Strike with only minor infractions on my record.

After I got back from Desert Strike, I was assigned to the post hospital. Luck was with me - Major Mullens was the detachment Commander and I had served with him in Korea.

Major Mullens wasn't too happy to see me. He said, "Woody, I knew you were insane in Korea. The stunt you pulled on Desert Strike takes the cake. The brass want your butt. Since you saved my rear in Korea I will do my best save your stripes.

Major Mulleins said, "Get your butt over and report to the chief nurse. Colonel Brown is her name and she is a tough old biddie."

My new boss was Colonel Brown who I had served with at Fort Carson, Colorado.

The Colonel welcomed me with open arms. The Colonel said, "Woody, I am glad to have you as my Trouble Shooter. Sorry to hear about your troubles on Desert Strike, but if you straighten out the O.B. for me you can forget the court martial.

Major Jones is the ward nurse and you will have her full support. Go to supply and draw your whites and report to Major Jones."

When I reported in the next morning I was shocked to see the hall lined with pregnant women waiting their turn for the delivery room. The ward was a mad house. I thought the women were being tortured by all the moans and screams.

Major Jones insisted that I watch a delivery. It was a good thing I had a good strong stomach. The delivery room was like a slaughter house. Blood was everywhere. After I watched the delivery I called Colonel Brown and said "thanks for ruining my love life." She said to hang in there and I would get used to it. I thought like hell I will.

At coffee break Major Jones and the other ward personnel had a good laugh at my discomfort in the delivery room. The second day I made new ward rules and posted them on the ward.

I made my first mistake when I told a new mother that all new babies were ugly. She broke into tears. After the women delivered they were sent to ward after two hours. They had been waited on. Every whim and wish were granted before I made my new rules.

The new rules I made stated that the patients would get their water, make their own beds and mop around their beds.

Most of the patients followed my new rules without complaining. Colonel Sims' wife was the only one raising hell. She stated she had a maid to do the dirty work at home. My answer was "you aren't at home now. Take your complaints to management."

When my second day was over, Colonel Brown and Major Jones came into my office. Both had smiles on their faces. Colonel Brown said, "Congratulations you have started a rank war. Colonel Sims came to see me today, complaining about the way you treated his wife. I set him straight - there is no rank on the wards. I can see changes already — the moral is higher and the wards are cleaner."

One month later I was informed the Chief nurse of the Army was coming for an inspection and wanted to see me personally.

The General's name was Chase and the word was she was a tough old girl. Colonel Brown said not to worry, the General was tough but fair. The day of judgment came and I was meeting my maker -General Chase. She was a woman who immediately got your attention. She was five feet tall and weighed one hundred pounds and was ramrod straight.

I was shaking in my shoes when I reported to the General. I stared at her opened mouth and felt like I had swallowed a bale of cotton. The General complimented us on how the wards looked. She stated that we had broke the record for deliveries. She said it must be the water and laughed.

General Chase dismissed Colonel Brown and Major Jones. She said, "I want to talk to Woody one on one." I thought she was throwing the outhouse at me.

After the Colonel and Major left General Chase said "sit and light up." "Woody, you have stepped into deep do-do. I am behind you one hundred percent. I have ripped up your court-martial and don't worry about the Surgeon General for he is senile. Besides you and I have something in common. I was a P.O.W of the Japanese."

The Preacher and the Adulteress

Bart Country

People were saying that Ruthevelyn Key wasn't what she pretended to be—a prim and proper school teacher and church pianist. She didn't fool them, so they weren't surprised when she was caught almost in the act of adultery. She was seen leaving a cheap Meridian hotel one morning before dawn with Bubba Amerson. Everyone was whispering—every layer of social standing; her church people, members of other churches and those who never went to church.

Sorely troubled, the Reverend Philemon Larkin stood on an early morning street corner in the West Alabama town of Red Pond, waiting for a long line of mule-drawn cotton wagons to pass. The good pastor, a tall sinewy man with bony facial contours and a slouch to his shoulders, was wearing faded blue bib over-alls, a patched blue chambray shirt and a greasy, soot smeared leather apron—the mark of his trade, the town's blacksmith. On thin, gray, close-cropped hair he wore a sweat-stained battered brown felt hat.

He was thinking: I reckon I'm a man of average intelligence, the town blacksmith and the pastor of The Valley Gospel Church. I don't cotton on to what the people are saying. I know in my heart she is a good woman ... I can't believe she did what they're saying.

He waited, unaware of the hazy saffron sun rising out of the trees across the river, casting long black shadows over the road and shooting silky golden streaks through the alleys between the buildings.

So lost in thought, he didn't hear the "Good mawning, Reverend, Suh" of the black teamsters driving the creaking jangling wagons that lumbered down River Street. As they turned left on Chockaloosa Road toward the gin, dust rose from the plodding feet of the mules and the squealing wheels of the wagons. Specks of hay and tiny wisps of cotton fibers danced in the slanting yellow rays that flickered through the slowly rotating wheel spokes. The preacher's mind was on Ruthevelyn Key and the vicious gossip surrounding her.

When the last wagon had rumbled past, he stepped off the wooden sidewalk into the shoe-top deep dust, crossed the street and quickly

63

walked the half block to the hardware store. As he entered the open doors, the odor of iron goods, leather and feed grain wrapped around him—the pleasant remembered smells of a lifetime. He paused for his eyes to become accustomed to the gloom.

Flemmon Griggs, owner of the hardware store, moved quickly from behind the counter to greet his pastor, grabbed his hand and said, "Good mornin', Brother Phil." Smiling while pumping the store keeper's hand, the preacher said, "Good mornin' to you, Brother Griggs." "What can I do for you Brother Phil?"

"I'm runnin' low on shoe nails. I'd sure "preciate it if you'd get your man to haul me a keg down to the forge."

"He's across the river this mornin'...took a load of to the old Smitherman place; uh, this afternoon be all right?"

"Sure ... fine. I got enough for a while ... don't want to run out. If this war lasts much longer, theys gonna be hard to come by. I pray that President Wilson finds a way to end this terrible war before our boys start gettin' killed. Hear tell that General Pershing and the first bunch of dough-boys has already landed in France."

The storekeeper wasn't thinking about the war this morning. Anxious to change the subject and looking embarrassed, he stammered, "Uh ... uh ... uh, Reverend?" "Yes, suh." "You heard any of the talk that's goin' 'round?"

Looking him in the eyes, the preacher said, "I'm mighty sorry to say I've heard some. I don't pay no mind to waggin, tongues, though." "Well, I think you'd better pay some mind to the latest. They's some in the church talkin' 'bout callin' a special meetin' after services Sunday to ..." "It's they right..."

"...to see 'bout writin' Sister Ruthevelyn out of the church." "Well now, Brother Griggs, nothin' like that's ever happened since I was called to preach. Now, I allows as that kind of judgin' is for the Lord to do." "Well, they may be somethin'in that..." "They most certainly is somethin, in that, Brother Griggs. It's plain, right there in the seventh chapter of Matthew...the first verse, as a matter of fact."

Brother Griggs met the preacher's gaze and then looked away at some invisible thing over his shoulder and quietly said, "I just thought you oughta know ..."

As he turned to leave the store, the preacher said, "Much obliged to you Brother Griggs", and stopping with his back to the storekeeper, he said, "You pray for me, now."

When the preacher came out of the hardware store, a group of men, who had gathered in front of the drugstore next door, rushed at him—jostling each other and all talking at the same time. He smiled, held up a hand and waited for them to settle down.

They scuffed their feet, looked sheepish and waited for Jearl Millen, a cotton farmer from the river bottom, to do the talking. He moved to the front, faced the preacher and said, "Reverend ... what are you ... uh ... goin' to do about ... ah, Sister Key'?" "Do about Sister Key? What ... uh? Why, they's nothin, to do. I mean ... it's not our place to..."

"But Preacher, somebody's gotta do somethin'. We can't have that kinda carryin' on ... her the church's piano player and ... and a school teacher, too. We..."

"What carryin' on, Brother Jearl?"

"Uh ... you know..."

"I don't know nothin", said the preacher.

"Well, know this, Brother Larkin. We are callin' a special meeting of the congregation after church Sunday, to..."

"You have that right," the preacher softly said. He glanced over their heads at the Tombigbee River, where most of the morning fog had melted away, leaving a few thready streaks of mist hugging the surface of the river.

Having become very quiet the men just stared at their pastor, who, after looking each man in the eyes, repeated, "You have that right." Touching his fingers to the brim of his hat and nodding, he said, "Good mornin', Brothers...uh, Y'all pray for me."

After the regular church services, the pastor remained in the pulpit looking down at his flock; his mind still singing the closing hymn:

> "Jesus keep me near the cross,
> There a precious fountain.
> Free to all a cleansing stream
> Flows from Calvary's mountain."

There on the front row sat twenty year old Ruthevelyn Key, small and chubby, staring straight ahead, dressed in Sunday clothes: a navy blue, broadcloth, floor length skirt, white cotton blouse, navy blue patent leather shoes and a small wide-brimmed hat with a black veil that hung down across the bridge of her nose. Her carefully brushed, long brown hair was parted in the middle, plaited and wound into two coils on each side of her head. Though she wore jewelry at other times, she never wore it in church.

Because of the controversy that surrounded her, she chose not to play for the services that day. With everybody whispering and staring, she just couldn't.

Clearing his throat, the Reverend Larkin said, "If there is no objection, before I turn the meetin' over to Brother Jearl, I would like to say somethin'." Looking out over the congregation he had served and loved for nine years, he listened with displeasure at their nervous fidgeting and irate whispering. Yes, he surely did love them. Waiting for the resentment in his heart to leave, he closed his eyes, raised his face to heaven and said a silent prayer: "Heavenly Father, I need your help. What am I gonna say? Please, Father, show your humble servant the way."

He waited; his faith so strong that he knew God would provide the answer. Like a blinding light in his head, it came to him what <u>he</u> was to say.

He opened his eyes and said, "Dear Hearts, open your Bibles and turn with me to the Gospel of John—chapter eight, verse three. He waited until the sibilant rustling of Bible pages stopped; and then, barely audible. he began to read:

"And the scribes and Pharisees brought unto Him a woman taken in adultery; and when they had set her in the midst; They say unto Him, Master, this woman was taken in adultery, in the very act.

Now Moses in the law commanded us, that such should be stoned: but what sayest Thou?" This they said, tempting Him, that they might have to accuse Him. But Jesus stooped down, and with His finger wrote on the ground, as though He heard them not.

"So when they continued asking Him, He lifted up Himself, and said unto them, 'He that is without sin among you, let him first cast a stone at her'."

And again He stooped down, and wrote on the ground. And they which heard it, being convicted by their own conscience, went out one by one, beginning at the eldest, even unto the last: and Jesus was left alone, and the woman standing in the midst. When Jesus had lifted up Himself, and saw none but the woman, He said unto her, "Woman where are those thine accusers? Hath no man condemned thee?" She said, "no man, Lord." And Jesus said unto her …

(Here the preacher abandoned his soft gentle voice and roared.)

"NEITHER DO I CONDEMN THEE: GO AND *SIN NO MORE!*" Jolted into shock by their pastor's sudden change in volume, the congregation began to squirm in their seats, uneasily waiting for him to continue. He wiped his face with both hands, smiled at them leaned forward and softly said,

"Loved ones, can we do less than our beloved Savior? … Can we?"

"I'm goin' to ask you all to bow your heads and look into your hearts, and if you can say, if you can truly say, that you are without sin, please remain seated. Y'all will be the only ones fit to judge. I suggest the others leave, and I'll turn the meetin' over to Brother Jearl." Again the preacher prayed silently to God, asking Him to place His hand on the congregation.

There was a moment of silence; then he heard someone get up and quickly walk out, followed by the rustle and rush of many leaving the church. When the shuffling of feet were no longer heard, the preacher opened his eyes to an empty church—empty except for Ruthevelyn Key—and said, "Amen!" Ruthevelyn looked up at the preacher and smiled. In a quiet voice she said, "Brother Phil, let me explain … to …"

"Honey, you don't need to explain nothin' to me. I don't judge you…"

…"But, Brother Phil, that really was me coming out of that hotel in Meridian. We had …"

"Honey, I still don't judge you. I leave that to the Lord. If you did what they say you did, in the eyes of God you are married … That's what I believe. A marriage license is just a piece of paper." "That's just it, Brother Phil, we are married. Bubba called me from Camp Shelby and said he had to see me right then…meet him in Meridian … he said it couldn't wait. I packed and got on the train that day.

When we met he told me his outfit was being shipped to Fort Dix, New Jersey, then they were going to France. We got married at the city hall and I was to go and be with him at Fort Dix till he shipped out. I'm leaving tonight."

"You know these people will think you're runnin' away don't you"?

"I don't care what they think … They'll think what they want to anyway … no matter what I do."

"Sure, you're right, Honey. Still, I wish you could stay with us."

"I have to go be with Bubba … be with him the short time we have left before he goes to France. You'll never know how much I thank you…how thankful I am to God for sending you to us. God bless you."

She dabbed at her eyes with a little blue handkerchief, smiled at him and said, "I love you; please keep praying for us … for Bubba. Good bye…"

Virgie and Rip
Bart Country

A big coal truck rumbled over the bridge across Five Mile Creek in Spradlin Hollow under which Virgil Ray and Ripley McGee were sprawled. Dirt, dust and gravel shook down into the Boone's Farm wine they were drinking.

Virgie and Rip were out-of-work coal miners in their thirties—out of work by choice because sitting under the bridge telling lies to each other and drinking cheap wine was more fun than loading coal, and a hell of a lot easier. Virgie sneezed while slapping at a wasp flying around his head and muttered, "Damn wasp dandruff."

After the truck had passed Rip said, "Wasp dandruff? Who in hell ever heard of wasp dandruff? You betta cut that out, Virgie ... people gonna think you done gone crazy."

"I don't care what they gonna think, Rip. It's gonna make me rich and famous. You just wait." "O.K. Virgie, I sho' God want to hear this. Whatcha gonna do?"

"You know Rip ... all this stuff goin', round and people snifflin, and sneezin' and the doctors don't know from beans what's causin' it. Oh, hell yeah, they says evvybody is allergic to one thang er another an'it makes they eyes water and they sneezes. What t'hell they know? Well, I tell you it could just as well be from wasp dandruff as anythin' else."

"O.K. Virgie, now you tell me how a wasp gonna have dandruff when they ain't got no hair. Now you tell me that."

Well, Mister Smartie-pants Rip, you ain't so smart. You ever look close at a wasp?" "Hell no, I ain't an'I ain't gonna. I got betta sense than to mess aroun, with them waspes. I ain't hankerin' to git myself stung. What kinda fool goes aroun' checkin' on wasp hairs, anyway?"

"Well, Mister Fraidy-Cat, if you looked at as many waspes as I have, you would know that evvy one of them's got two hairs growin, out they heads. I allows as how it only takes one hair to make dandruff. You add up all the hairs on a bunch of waspes on a wasp nest and you gonna sho as hell git wasp dandruff. I guarantee it."

Rip reached for the Boone's Farm wine bottle, lifted it to his mouth and took a swallow. "Aaaah", he said, "Man that's good stuff. They ain't much left ... here, you drank the rest."

"Eh, you go 'head an, drank it. They's another bottle in that croaker sack over yonder."

Rip drained the bottle and wiped his mouth on the back of his sleeve as an old car rattled over the bridge sending down more dust and dirt. He sat for a while staring at Virgie while the wine took effect. Nodding his head, he said, "You know, Virgie, evvy now an, then you do make a little sense. You just the kind what's gonna git rich off a buncha fools. Now tell me how you gonna do it."

"I ain't got it all worked out yet but I been thinkin'. You know they's a lotta folks who will believe anything. That's what I'm countin' on ... Let me git that other bottle and I'll tell you what I got in mind."

He stumbled over to the sack and yanked out another bottle of wine. He rummaged around in the sack and pulled out a bag of Golden Flake corn-chips and said, "You want any these corn chips? It's all we got to eat. They's good but they ain't much of 'em. All they's good fer is to make you hungry."

While digging in the sack he muttered to himself, "I thought I had a hunk of baloney in here but I don't. You sure you don't want some of these corn-chips?" "Naw, but I'll take some of that wine." Virgie handed him the bottle while stuffing the cornchips into his mouth and said, "This ain't much of a dinner. We gone have to find us some real food. I'm 'bout starved."

When he had swallowed the last corn-chip he reached over and took the bottle from Rip and gulped a long swig. He slid closer and poked him lightly in the belly and said, "This is what I got in mind. We'll show this on the TV ... We'll show this doctor's office or some kinda laboratory or somethin' like that ... Lotsa lights blinkin, an' bottles an'thangs bubblin'... Then a cute little blon' lookin' thang— looks kinda like Dolly Partin—comes in battin' her eye-lashes and says, 'Here Doctor, here's the last hundred waspes. Now we can make the wasp dandruff medicine.' They dump 'em in this thang that looks like a little bitty whiskey still and throws a switch. Directly a few drops comes out t'other endand drips in a little jar-like hickey."

"Them drops are gold-colored an' shines like a light. The doctor holds it up an, in a spooky kinda voice says, 'This is it...It's worth its weight in diamon's. We'll call it ... Let's call it VIRGIE'S SNEEZE BEGONE!'"

"Then somebody real famous ... like Senator Ted Kennedy or Rush Limbaugh or Minnie Pearl ... or somebody like that holds up a bottle of the stuff an' says how wonderful it is - how it stopped they runny noses. Then evvybody gonna run down to Wal-Mart or Big B drug store an' buy lem out...An' that's how I'm gonna be rich.,"

Half asleep, Rip nodded his head and said, "Makes sense to me, but it's gonna take lotsa money to git this thang goin'. How you gonna swang that?" Virgie turned over on his side and said,

"That's the hardes' part an' I ain't figgered that out yet."

"Well, you betta figger out how we gonna eat today."

"Yeah, you right." "Say, who's that sittin' down there by the creek?" asked Rip. Virgie stood up to look and said, "Oh, that's ol' Nathan Shipps." "Wonder what t'hell he's doin' down there?"

Virgie said, "Looks to me like he's readin' his Bible. That's what he's usually doin'. Let's go down there an' see if he'll give us a job sweepin' his yard or cuttin, his grass or somethin,."

They stumbled down to the creek bank and Virgie called out,

"Hey there, Brother Nate. Whatcha doin'?" "Well, I been sittin' here readin' my Bible an' thinkin' 'bout that time, right over there by that there rock, that time of the big baptizin', when Doreen Sledge committed blasphemy in the middle of that creek. Pore Brother Willbanks...I felt so shamed for him." Rip said, "Why is it evvybody allus pointin, at that place an' saying what a terrible thang Doreen did. Lotta folks sayin' it that ain't no better'n her.', Nathan said, "Well, I reckon you right. We ain't s'posed to judge. Uh, what'ch you boys doin'?"

"We was wonderin, do you got some work you wanted us to do...Iike cut yore grass or split some wood or somethin' an'—we ain't et today an' we shore would like to do some chores fer a meal, an'..."

"I ain't got nothin, but I tell you what. Miz Brakefield, over 'crost the creek, might let y'all have a meal ... wo'nt even have to do no work. Hear tell that all she asks is fer you to say a Bible verse."

Vergie shook his head and said, "I heared that too, but the thang is I can only 'member one verse … 'Jesus wept' an' that's 'cause it's the shortest verse in the Bible. Say, you readin' the Bible. Tell us one we can say."

Nathan looked at them intently. He was holding his Bible in his left hand with his index finger keeping his place. He said, "I been readin, here 'bout Samson an' Delilah…hmmm let's see; I reckon you can say this: 'And Samson found a jaw bone of an ass, and put forth his hand and took it, and slew a thousand Philistines'—Judges15:15. You think y'all can 'member that?"

Rip repeated it a couple of times and said, "I b'lieve I got it now. Come on, Virgie, let's go. I'm 'bout to starve."

They hurried up the bank to the road, turned tight and walked around a curve and up a hill to where Mrs. Brakefield lived—a small white clapboard house trimmed in red with a white picket fence around it. Virgie reached out and pulled Rip to a stop and said, "Rip, you the one what knows the verse. You go 'round to the back and tell it to Miz Brakefield an' I'll wait here by the gate. Rip nodded his head a couple of times and said,

"That's a good idee… O.K., here I go. Wish me luck."

He bent over, unlatched the gate, opened it and walked through. Almost running, he hurried to the back along a gravel walk lined with zinnias and knocked on the door frame. He heard the sound of someone coming to the door. It opened and the heart-stopping aroma of frying chicken hit him in the face like a slap. A small, sweet-faced woman with white curly hair, pink cheeks and wearing a baby-blue apron to match her eyes said,

"Why … hello, Ripley. How are you?"

"I do tollable, Miz Brakefield. How, re you?" "I'm just fine, Ripley. What can I do for you?" "Well, Miz Brakefield, me an' my buddy, Virgie…er, we was wonderin, if you had some work fer us to do…to do fer a meal, an' we…"

"No Ripley, but I never turn anybody away—that is, if he can quote me a Bible verse. Can you do that?"

"Yes'm, I b'lieve I can." By this time Rip had become weak in the knees and almost mesmerized by the delicious smells coming from Mrs. Brakefield's kitchen. She smiled sweetly and said, "Now Ripley, let's hear it."

He held on to the door frame for support, took a deep breath and almost passed out from an overdose of fried chicken smell and blurted out, "Samson took the jaw bone of a mule and knocked the asses off a thousan' Philadelphians."

Mrs. Brakefield stared at him and turned white while holding her breath. Then she let out a loud whoop and started laughing; her complexion went from white to scarlet while tears ran down her face. Weak with laughter and unable to stand on her feet, she slowly slid to the floor, clutching the door. She rocked back and forth, hugging her stomach and making gurgling, sobbing sounds.

Terrified, Rip forgot the fried chicken, raced to the front yard and called out to Virgie, "Come here, Virgie! Quick! Somethin' done happent to Miz Brakefield … She's havin a fit!"

They hurried around to the back where Mrs. Brakefield had recovered and was sitting on the top step wiping eyes on her apron. She said, "Hello, Virgil; help me up and y'all come in and let's see if I can come up with something for Y'all to eat."

Loubertha at the Welfare Office

Bart Country

It was close to five o'clock and the welfare office almost deserted when Loubertha Sledge struggled in with her four children. Mrs. Feeny, the office manager, met her in the middle of the room, glared at her and said, "Couldn't you get here any earlier?"

"They said git chere befo five o'clock and Ahys hyere befo five o'clock."

Mrs. Feeney pointed to a glass enclosed cubicle and said "Well, go in there and Miss Angelo will take your application." Then she turned and locked the door against further quitting-time intrusions.

Holding her baby in her lap, Loubertha sat in a metal folding chair across from Miss Angelo. Her other children gathered close around her while she waited for Miss Angelo's questions. Miss Angelo said,

"What is your name?"

"My name is Loubertha Sledge."

Miss Angelo looked over her glasses and said,

"Are you related to Doreen Sledge?"

"Yeah, she's my sister. How come you know Doreen? She ain't got no children".

"Oh, we know her all right. You don't have to have children to come here".

Miss Angelo then asked for and typed all the other routine information required of welfare applicants. She sighed, looked up and said,

"Ms. Sledge, all I need now is information about your children. Let's start with the baby.

How old is she?"

"Tin month oll."

"What's her name?"

"She name Helen Sue Abernathy. Huh daddy is Rev Abernathy, our pastuh."

Miss Angelo typed this, pointed to the next child and "What's her name and how old is she?"

"She three yair oil. Huh name is Bonnie Benefield. Huh daddy is Rev. Benefield, our pastor befo Rev. Abernathy-"

Miss Angelo looked up to heaven, released an even heavier sigh and pointed at the little boy.

"He name John Wayne Collins. He is six yair oil.
His daddy is Rev. Collins, our pastuh befo Rev. Benefield."

Tappity-tap-tap went the angry typewriter. Miss Angelo, shaking her head, just looked at the last child Loubertha said, "He tin yair ol'.
His name is Lucious."

Miss Angelo waited a few seconds and asked, what's his father's name?"

"Well, "Loubertha said, "Ah don't know. That was befo Ah got saved."

Preacher Man

Woody

Some old-timers were sitting around the bus depot reading handbills that a preacher had put up around the town.

Judge Stringfellow was reading them to Jug Tedder and Nip Yeager, his drinking buddies, when he stopped and said "Jug, how about givin' me a dip o'yore snuff an I'll read you all these here posters. Boys, according to this one here' that preacher man has done some big miracles. He's cured old lady Culpepper's lumbago and now she is dancing down at Old Sawmiller's Saloon over in Fayette County. Says here that there was a man who ain't walked in years and that preacher laid his hands on him and said, 'Brother, you can throw that wheelchair away'. Believe it, the man got up and did a buck dance."

Nip said, "Who in the hell b'lieves all that crap?"

Judge said, "We'll just have to go and see this here preacher man for ourselves.

Jug looked serious as he tapped the Judge on his chest and said, "Ju ... judge ... uh... do you think he ... he c...c...can cu... cu... cure m m my st...stuttering"?

Judge said, "Jug, we can shore give it a try ... ain't gonna hurt nothin'to go and see iffin them posters is true, you'll be talking the horns offen a billy goat. What about you, Nip?

You got any other problem, ceptin drinkin'hard likker?"

Yeah, Judge...I have...uh, but I don't wanna talk about it.

Well, Nip, you take anoyher slug of yore likker an, you ain't gonna have no trouble talkin, bout nothin. Just what is this problem you got that you don't wanna talk about?

"It's like this, judge...uh ... my love life is deader'n a frozen woodpecker. I'm worried as hell, bout it." "Looky here, Nip. Iffin you can't perform after that there likker, it's shore gonna take a miracle."

The town was in a festive mood the day the circuit riding preacher was to begin a week of meetings to heal the sick and infirm. As the talk went around, the tales of his many miracles grew and grew.

Judge, Nip and Jug were among the first to arrive at the campgrounds where the services were to be held. Nip brought an ample supply of his likker. Jug brought a large can of Bruton snuff, and Judge furnished the brains along with his large ego.

Folding chairs had been set up in rows out in the open air; the three men parked themselves on the front row near the pulpit that the preacher had put up. They sat drinking, scratching, spitting and flailing at gnats that were swarming all over the campgrounds.

"These gnats are bad enough. I hope, them damn bitin'black flies don't swarm, "said Judge, as he took another slug of corn likker. "Nip, you'member that time you passed out under the bridge an'them flies sucked all yore blood out?"

"Hell yeah, I remember, Judge. Them damn flies almost kilt me."

Jug said, "It... it...sh...sh...shore is huh...hot. Luh...luh...let's g.g...go over yuh...yonder in the shade,"

"Pass the jug around an' we'll go fin'shade", said the Judge. "Hey looky over yonder under that big oak tree. Ain't that Widder Jones and Widder Smith? Let's go over there...they allus got a basket of good fried chicken'n biscuits." They moved over to the big oak tree and Widow Jones said, "Law, if it ain't the Judge and his friends! Y'all just set down and take the load off yore feet. Me and Adelle will have us some vittles later on. Hey Nip, Honey, whar's in that jug you got there? Y'all already been drinking, so let me and Adelle have a snort and try to catch up with y'all."

Nip pulled the cob out of the jug, passed it to Widow Jones and said, "Now you take it easy on my likker. It's got a kick like a saw mill mule." Widow Jones took a big swallow. Her face turned red, then white. Tears came into her eyes as she she regained her breath she licked her lips and said "Boy, that was some good stuff!"

Off in the southwest storm clouds were building 'unnoticed by the people at the camp ground. The preacher arrived with his hangers on and they set up the loud-speakers. The crowd was growing larger—talking excitedly under the big tree, Judge, Nip and Jug were feeling no pain. Jug had paired off with Widow Jones, Nip had a lip lock on Widow Smith and Judge was getting cozey with the basket that held the fried chicken. The meeting had started, and while a Blue-grass band played gospel music, the collection plate was passed around—a big straw hat instead of a plate. The preacher was shouting and praying, "Praise the Lord! Give till you hurt."

Judge said, "Hell, I'm already hurtin'…damn gnats in my my eyes … gnats in my ears … gnats in my. I'll bet that big mouth preacher inhales a swarm o'them gnats." Collection hat came by and Nip put in a dollar and took out change for a twenty and said, "Amen … the Lord giveth and the Lord taketh away."

Storm clouds were looking ugly and rumbling closer. Lightening flashed and thunder could be heard off in the distance.

The preacher said, "Lets move things on before the storm gets here. Put all your request for prayer on a piece of paper. Put 'em in the hat and I'll pray for a miracle for everyone." Judge, Nip, Jug and the widows, who were drinking and having a big party under the oak tree, put their prayer request in the hat and waited for their miracle to happen. Suddenly the rain came down in sheets and the crowd ran for cover. The preacher joined the Judge and his friends under the big oak tree, because during the service he had spotted the likker jug and the basket of chicken.

Nip offered the jug to the preacher and was not surprised when he accepted it. As the preacher put the jug to his lips, a bolt of lightening hit the big oak tree. Judge, Nip, Jug, the preacher and the widows lighted up like a Christmas tree. The jug melted in the preacher's hand.

The hair on the widow's head caught fire and only the rain saved them from premature baldness. The storm had scattered the congregation, so the healing service broke up. The next morning the Judge was down at the depot when Jug came in smiling and said "listen…Mary had a little lamb … the houn'dog runned after the rabbit…Iisten I can talk…listen… listen …"

The Judge almost fell off his stool. He slapped him on his back and said, "Well good for you!" Looking over Jug's shoulder at the door, he said "Where's Nip." Jug said, "You ain't gonna b'liev it. Him and them two widders caught that night train to Memphis."

Judge said, "what about that preacher … he alright?"

Jug laughed and said, "He had to have his teeth drilled out. That ther lightnin' bolt done fused his gold teeth together."

The moral of this story is that miracles do happen. Sometimes they happen in strange and mysterious ways.

Wild Ones

Perry Woodley

My brothers and I grew up in the Boldo community near Jasper, Alabama. We were considered normal kids by our mother and father, but our grandparents had a different idea. They thought we were possessed by the devil.

Lenton was the oldest, Harold the youngest; and since I was the middle one, I was the troublemaker. We did everything together- movies, swimming, fighting and team sports.

We walked to school and there was a lot of mischief for the three of us to get into. We all carried slingshots. Lenton was the best shot. He could knock squirrels out of trees. Harold was second best. I was the spotter who picked out their targets. Some of the targets I picked out got us in big trouble.

Every year when school started, neighbors along our route removed all breakables out of reach of our slingshots. Things were getting dull on our walks to and from school. I started a feud with the Sherer clan. There were five of the Sherer brothers, but Lenton's slingshot evened the odds. Things were lively for awhile, but boredom set in. Both families put their heads together to plan some mischief involving all of us.

The Pentecostal church was having a revival and we decided to attend. Dad said we could go if we behaved and stayed out of trouble.

The first night of the revival we bathed in the old swimming hole. Mother checked to make sure we were clean and had washed behind our cars. I have never figured out why mothers check ears and nothing else. Our slingshots were taken away. Mom said they wouldn't look good in church.

We met the Sherers at Poley Creek and walked to church with them. They had also been warned by their parents to act civilized.

When we arrived at the church a good crowd was already there. It was the fall of the year- hot, dry and dusty. Air conditioners were unheard of back then, so all the windows and doors were open. The congregation used fans made of cardboard to fan themselves. The fans carried advertisements for the local funeral homes.

Soon after we were seated the services started. The shouting and praising of the Lord could be heard for miles. Some of the good sisters fainted. The Preacher said they were touched by the spirit, but I believe it was from the heat and dust. The shouting and praising went on til midnight. On our way home we began to try to figure out ways to shorten the services. Someone said we could shout "fire". We quickly ruled against shouting fire. Someone mentioned a yellow-jacket nest he had found. We immediately got the idea of capturing the yellow-jackets and turning them loose inside the church. The Sherer clan and me came up with a plan to capture and release the yellow-jackets inside the church.

The third night of the revival we decided to put the neck of a gallon wine jug in the opening of the yellow-jacket nest.

On the way home that night we detoured by the yellow jacket nest. I carefully put the neck of the wine jug into the nest. The next morning we went by the nest to check on our project. The jug was full of very angry yellow jackets. We carefully removed the jug and capped it. A small air hole was made in the cap and the jug was placed in a shade. We were ready to put our plan into effect that night.

As we were walking to church that night, we decided to release the yellow jackets when the congregation was going down to the altar to be saved.

When we arrived at church, it was packed. The big crowd suited us just fine. The congregation was making their way down the aisle shouting and praising the Lord. The cap was removed from the jug and rolled down the aisle among the congregation. Out of the jug spewed a yellow stream of misery.

Soon the people were slapping their bodies in a frenzy. The good sisters were trying to come out of their clothes and people were rolling on the floor trying to get away from the yellow jackets. During the riot, we left the church on the run.

The next day we heard that a record number of sinners had been saved.

Fighting Fire

Ramonia Evans

My husband had always forbidden me to burn our trash since we live in the country in a no fire protection area, and he considers me to be an absolute scatterbrain. However, he did not get around to burning it himself as often as was needed, and since I consider him to be overly cautious, almost to the point of paralysis, I developed this plan. When I noticed the trash barrel was about one-third full, I would burn it. Jim never noticed, and I did not have to nag him to burn the trash.

One fall day, I took my trash out, set it afire, and went into the house to get ready for the 1 p.m. to 9 p.m. shift I was scheduled to work at J. C. Penny that day. I was humming along, combing my hair and putting on make-up when I glanced out my bedroom window. To my horror the yard was on fire!! A breeze had come up and blown the burning trash out of the barrel and caught the dry grass and leaves on fire.

I had to put it out before it got to my husband's much loved red Volkswagon, which it was inching towards. I had to save the car, I had to save the woods, I had to save any credibility I was ever to have with my husband, when he saw all of this.

I grabbed the first shoes I saw, which were high-heeled pumps, threw on a blazer from the chair, and grabbed a blanket and ran out to fight fire. I jammed the top on the burn barrel, and began beating out the flames with the blanket. This worked well, but I noticed the flames had gotten under the V.W. What to do now?! I was so afraid the fire would make the gas tank explode. Then the situation would be totally out of control.

I had either to let the car burn up, and Jim would kill me, or get down and put the fire out, and a possible explosion may kill me. I picked the latter. I managed to get the flames put out, and stood up and surveyed the mess. There was a black charred place almost as big as our house. I decided that maybe I could hide it, as I knew it would be dark when he got home. It was supposed to rain the next day, and maybe some of it would wash away.

Desperate times call for desperate measures —so I went to the barn and got two bales of hay, and spread it all over the black, especially under the V.W. I stood back and I looked, and it didn't look bad... I felt so grimy and itchy, I took a good look at myself. There I stood a true come-as-you-are firefighter ... wearing a bra, pantyhose, high-heeled shoes, a corduroy blazer and hay! I laughed so hard I cried. It was a good thing we did live in the woods, considering my strange garb. I began to think *Jim* may have a point, about that scatterbrained business. At any rate I went directly in the house and called Dixie Waste Disposal and registered for trash pick up. Jim, bless his heart, never did mention the black yard covered with hay!

Just Not My Day

Jessie Abbott Sherer

It was one of those wet dreary Saturday mornings. I was moving at a fast trot for I had a dozen or so errands to run before I went into work at 4:00PM. It seemed that I never had one of those slow-paced, take-your-own-sweet-time mornings.

I had packed, wrapped and addressed four or five packages to mail to my Marine son Lee, in Vietnam. I always kept the packages five pounds or less. That way the postman would stamp SAM in great big capital letters and they would be shipped, "Same As Air Mail," on a space available basis.

As I stepped inside the post office there was a sign that said, "Slippery When Wet." There were puddles of water standing where the rain had blown in as the doors were opened.

The post office closed at noon on Saturdays and there was already a long line waiting in fron of two windows, the third window was closed. I had started for the shortest line when I heard the third window opening and there stood a man motioning for some of us to come to his window.

Well, I changed direction in a hurry and to my dismay I found out fast how right that sign, "Slippery When Wet," was. The next thing that I know, I am sliding across the floor as though I am sliding for home plate after hitting that winning run. I guess I managed to jump up almost as fast as I fell.

I had mailed so many packages that all the postal workers knew my name and he was saying, "Mrs. Abbott are you O K? Are you sure that you're not hurt?" After brushing myself off I managed to say, "Yes, I'm O K, just my pride is hurt a little." In the meantime, the people were helping to gather my packages.

Believe it or not, but no one made an effort to step in front of me in that line. I think they figured that I had earned that spot as first in line.

Honest, I think that if anyone had tried to step in front of me while I was on the floor, I would have bitten them on the leg! That thought actually crossed my mind and my gnashing teeth were ready. That

83

was my territory and I would have protected it! I had earned it with the humilation of that slide across the floor and with my wet bottom.

This just wasn't going to be my day. While I was mailing my packages it had started raining much harder. When I reached the car my key would not unlock the door. I stood there fumbling with the keys trying each one, but none of them would work. I glanced around and there was a man sitting in his car just laughing and shaking his head. I glanced in the other direction and about three cars down the line sits another car identical to the one that I'm trying to get into. It finally dawns on me that the other car must be mine. So, with the man still watching me, I nonchantly walked over to the other car and tried the key. Like magic, the key worked.

I could just hear that man going home and telling his wife about the stupid woman standing in the torrential rain trying to get in the wrong car. "The poor soul didn't know her own car!"

In my defense, the cars were absolutely identical and parked about three spaces apart. It could happen to anyone!

The Hungry Burglar

Jessie Abbott Sherer

Honestly, I would never begrudge a hungry person a bite of any food that I might have on hand. If I thought a person was hungry, I would willingly share my food with them. All they need to do is ask for the food.

They don't have to break my windows out and come in and burglarize my house while I am gone. When they start messing around and destroying and trashing my property-then I get a bit perturbed.

One Sunday afternoon I returned home after being gone just about two hours. My daughter-in4aw and her daughter almost let me go into the house alone-but at the last moment they decided that they could stay for a couple of minutes.

I unlocked the door and stepped inside and had only taken a couple of steps when I noticed papers, books, and old mail scattered all over the floor. Then I noticed that my 25-inch screen TV set was missing and a lamp or two had been turned over. I yelled-took a couple more steps where I could see through the kitchen and the back door was standing wide open- well I really yelled because I knew good and well that I did not leave my door standing open. I had started back through the house when Kim grabbed my arm and said, "Come on, let's get out of here, don't touch anything." With one of them dragging me and the other one shoving me, they got me to the front door when Roxie Baby, my little "Peek-A-Poo" came out of hiding. I stooped down and picked her up and took her out with me.

Kim had her cell phone and she called 911. The dispatcher said, "We have just had another call about trouble on that street. There should be someone there shortly." One of our neighbors on a side street had seen the burglar driving off in my next door neighbor's car.

There are only five houses on this street and one of them is vacant. The other four are occupied by lone occupants in each house - three widows and a widower. Luckily, everyone was away that afternoon.

The burglar took a 22 rifle from the last house, a microwave oven from the next house, a car and a TV set from the next one, and my TV from my house. Not only that, but the burglar took time to lot a cantaloupe from my refrigerator and left the rind on my counter top. I had planned to have cantaloupe with a couple scoops of ice cream as my dessert that night. The burglar took care of that little deal though.

He took my long handled shovel to break the window out in my back bedroom. It had double panes and it took more than one lick to finally break through both panes.

The burglar is in jail under a $50, 000.00 bond. I have come to one of three conclusions-I haven't decided which one is accurate yet.

The young man is so egotistical that he thinks that he can outsmart all the law enforcement officers in the area, or number 2; he has to be downright stupid to pull some of the things that he has done or number 3, he is crying out for help-just begging to be caught and made to stop. As I say, I haven't decided which one it is yet.

He is denying taking anything except the car. But—two witnesses saw and talked to him out in Boldo and they say that he was in the stolen car and there was a micro oven and two TVs sitting on the back seat. The police were called but he was long gone by the time that they got there.

He took the car to a dealer in Haleyville trying to trade it in on another car. He left the car, along with his driver's license, with the dealer while he took the car for a test drive. The only thing, he never returned the car to the dealer.

He is stopped for speeding on 78 East and when the tag was run it had been reported as a stolen car. So. he was locked up. The police are hoping that his arrest will solve quite a few burglaries in the area. At several scenes the burglar has taken time to raid the fridge and at one place he took a pair of boots and left his old ones in their place. It is beginning to add up.

Super Girl and The Bicycle

Ramonia Evans

He walked along the street, head and shoulders hunched forward, hands clasped behind his back. He wore an old felt hat, and in winter, a shapeless overcoat. He glowered fiercely at everyone he met. His name was Fred Fowler, and he was one of the dreaded three bachelors that lived around the corner of our block.

Their house was tiny, painted yellow, and neat, as was their yard, but Oh, the things that went on in that house, as reported variously through our little girl-neighborhood-network.

The bachelors themselves were a scruffy group, with grey stubbled faces. They wore old bib-overalls, old hats and denim caps, as they sat on their three chairs, in the yard in front of their house. Whenever any of us little girls walked by, they would call to us to come over there, that they had quarters to give us. Of course we all ran away, shivering with fear.

Some little girls from farther away in the neighborhood, little girls not as knowing and wise as we, would occasionally go into their house for the quarters. We would hear wild tales of the bachelors having them dance and jump on the beds, so they could see their panties.

To my knowledge, none of us ever mentioned any of this to our Mothers. I don't really know why, I know I didn't tell my Mother because I didn't think she'd understand. Even at nine years old I thought Mother very unaware - naive about such things. I knew the version of the facts of life that she told me was very different from the information we passed, shocking each other with our whispers.

One morning Mother answered a knock at the door, and there stood old Fred Fowler! I stayed as close to Mom as I could, and heard him inviting her over to look at a bicycle he had for sale, that he wanted to sell her for my younger brother.

I heard Mom agree to come and look at it. I couldn't believe my ears, I just had to protect her someway. I had visions of the three bachelors trying to look at her panties. I could just see her jumping and dancing on their beds, terrified not to! I could see the three of them yelling and stomping and giving her quarters.

But there was no way I could explain this to my poor "innocent Mother" she just wouldn't understand. I begged and pleaded with her not to go, but to no avail. She felt my forehead, and looked at me like I'd taken leave of my senses, so when she started off, I followed her from a distance on the weed-patch side of the street. I cried all the way, and even more when she went into their house. I was right across the street, behind a tree. I was only nine, but I felt so powerful, because I thought they were going to hurt my Mom.

If she didn't come out in a few minutes, I was going to run in their house and tell them to unhand her, and I was going to kick them, and scratch them and bite them and scream as loud as I could. That was my plan to save Mother.

But luckily, it wasn't needed, she came out in about five minutes wheeling the bicycle. I was so relieved, that I thanked God right there for sparing my Mother. She wheeled the bike home, and I made my way back through the weed patch. She never knew I followed her or any of this.

This is the story of how I almost saved Mother from the evil bachelors. As long as she lived, I always felt I had to protect my Mother.

The Big Change

Betty Gallman

My immediate impression of the doctors suggestion was, "this is the end of the world for me". I had walked with crutches for over forty years. Never in my life had I felt more physically challenged than at that moment.

What the doc had recommended, after careful evaluation of my case, was to remove the right hip prosthesis. This meant I could no longer walk. They had already whacked on that hip enough. But the infection was bad and to get rid of it meant removing the hip and that meant cutting more off the femur. I'd be ole gimp for certain, now.

I would be able to take short walks using a walker. The crutches had done damage to my right elbow and ole Arthur was constantly bothering me. I had an electric scooter at home and now this would be my means of transportation.

I told the doc he could leave and to be certain that the door hit him in the ass on his way out. The nursing staff came around several times to check on me. I'd just smile and tell them I was fine. I just wanted to think about the situation. Finally, they decided to leave me a lone. Believe me, if I could have reached that doctor I would have given him a big right upper cut to the jaw despite the bad elbow.

The procedure was done and I was well on my way to mending. There were times I wanted to scream and cry, but I didn't.

I kept a stiff upper lip, as the ole saying goes and a smile on my face. Oh, there were times when I wanted to, and the Lord only knows what. Naw! I didn't want to kill myself. That would have made some people happy, I am certain. No, I wanted to stay around and just see what all I could do.

When I got home I started looking for a van with a lift. I found one. It was just the ticket. I could handle it pretty good, too. The only time I ever got disgusted was when I would go to Wal- Mart. You could never find a parking place. If I were able to find a place to park some nut case would park too close and I could not get in, or out for that matter. I left nasty notes on their cars like "thank you for not blocking my wheelchair lift" or "Have a nice day, by blocking my door". There was one incident where I was waiting for my friend to come out of the store and this car pulled in to a handicapped area. There was no proper tag or placard hanging from the rear view mirror. I got out and was about to open my big mouth when the door opened and a great big, wide, tall, mean looking woman stepped out and looked in my direction over her glasses. I just smiled and decided that I would leave that one a lone.

Lord only knows, that woman would have smashed me like a little ole bug. I turned my scooter around and went into the store by one door and went out the other door.

Things like shopping and just going in general take a little longer now because my mode of travel is different. And since then I have a ramp van with automatic doors, a power seat and hand controls with my special steering knob.

The bottom line for me now is that the scooter, better known as THE RASCAL, along with my new ramp van has enabled me to continue doing the things that I always did and possibly much more. I joined a writing group, a developmental disabilities support council, and I am very active in the many programs that protect the rights of people with disabilities. But the most important thing is I can take my water with me whenever I go anywhere. You see, my rascal has a basket and a cup holder. I never knew how liberating the basket on a scooter could be. Maybe one of these days I will try for my eighteen wheel license. Who knows what the future holds.

Sergeant Major Dane, USA

Betty Gallman

The big Army green bus traveled the long road from the terminal to the Base Barracks. The new recruits aboard the bus were tired and hot from their long trip.

Suddenly the bus stopped and Sergeant J. R. Kricket started his long speech to the new recruits. There were several other officers aboard the bus, one being Captain Min Pin Kasey from Pleasant Hill, Alabama.

While Sergeant Kricket was talking to all the recruits, Captain Kasey glanced out the side window and saw a figure standing at the edge of a cliff overlooking a waterfall.

Captain Kasey noticed that this figure had distinct physical features. The body frame was square, especially the head, and the body was muscular, giving the appearance of dignity and strength.

The eyes were medium, deep set and dark, displaying an intelligent expression. Ears were medium sized and the nose was well defined. Captain Kasey noticed that the figure was smiling, and the teeth were strong in appearance, well developed and clean. The skin was smooth and flawless and the exposed parts were tan. Captain Kasey watched as the figure walked away from the cliff; the gait displayed strength, power, and speed.

Captain Kasey was drawn back to the voice of Sergeant Kricket who was saying, "Your Commanding Officer, Sergeant Major G. Dane, is a force to be reckoned with and all of you recruits will soon realize this is a true statement. DISMISSED TO YOUR QUARTERS!"

All the new recruits left and went to the barracks. Captain Kasey went to Headquarters where she ran into an old friend, Lieutenant Roxie. Lieutenant Roxie had been at the base P. 1 for over three years. When the two had finished talking over times, Captain Kasey asked Lieutenant Roxie about the figure she had seen overlooking the cliff. Lieutenant Roxie smiled, "You mean Sergeant Major Dane."

He's been here for about five years. He is out going, friendly, and has a big mouth. His family been traced back to Greece as far back as

2000 B.C. The majority of the family comes from Germany where they were great hunters.

They came to the United States in the middle 18OO'S. One of his early ancestors, General Turk, lived with Buffalo Bill Cody. Sergeant Major Dane is big, fast, powerful, and courageous.

Yet, he can be gentle, affectionate, and protective. Sergeant Major also has inborn patience and understanding. Lieutenant Roxie went on to tell Captain Kasey that the Sergeant had health problems that were mostly orthopedic in origin. He would always need a soft surface to lie on to keep the calluses from forming. He needed to always eat nutritious food and get plenty of exercise. Captain Kasey learned that the Sergeant Major was tough when it came to training.

He was patient. He was resistant with the recruits, yet His temperament was spirited, courageous, friendly, dependable, never timid or aggressive. The more Captain Kasey thought about the description of Sergeant Major Dane the more she realized that the Sergeant Major displayed the qualities and appearance of her friend, a Great Dane Dog, named MAJOR.

The Wedding

Ramona Bowen Evans

Every girl dreams of a wedding that's different from any one else's. One that's uniquely her own. Upon reflection over the years, I believe that I truly achieved that goal! Jack and I met when I was fifteen and he was sixteen. I had quit school because of financial reasons at the end of the ninth grade. Jack's family had just moved to Council Bluffs, from Los Angeles, and I thought he was the most worldly and sophisticated boy that I had ever met. The fact that he was very handsome didn't hurt either. He had black hair, hazel green eyes and a nice lean physique. He was six feet tall, had wonderful manners, was never crude, and every inch a gentleman. He was at the end of the eleventh grade. I worked at a dry cleaners and laundry and Jack thought I was grownup and exciting because I didn't go to school and had a job and my own money. I made minimum wage— a whole 65 cents an hour.

We were "In Love!" We were so much alike, both stubborn and hard headed and each wanted to have the last word. We fought about everything, including what color our bedroom walls would be when we got married.(He said chocolate brown-I said, no way!). Each of us was jealous of the other. One time he poured tomato juice on my head because I was gone too long with his sister. One time he was going to a basketball game with his buddies when I wanted to go to a movie; while he was taking a shower I put all of his Levi's in his mom's washer so they'd all be wet. He went to the game anyway and wore them wet. Despite our childish antics we were crazy about each other. We would break up and I would throw my engagement ring in the yard or he would throw it in the toilet. We'd tell his younger brothers and sisters if they found it they could just keep it. Of course, by the time the poor kids found it we'd be all made up and take it back. We always knew though that we would marry someday. Everytime we said we would marry the next spring. And every year something came up. His job would run out (he was a painter). One time my mother fell and broke her leg and I wouldn't leave her. One spring he really didn't know if he wanted to marry and one time it was me, that wasn't sure. But that was fine with both of us. Actually I guess neither one of us felt ready to be so grown up.

Our backgrounds were very different. Jack came from a large, noisy open family and his parents were very young. They were not conservative people, to put it mildly. He was the oldest of nine children. All of those names started with "J". The last little girl, Janet, was born when he was nineteen years old. I loved to go over there because there was always something going on and they accepted me as just another one of the kids. The two younger ones, when they were grown, told me that sometimes they couldn't remember if Jack was their brother or if I was their sister. They were born after we started dating. There were three members of my family. Myself, mother, and my brother Ralph, who joined the Navy the week he turned seventeen. I worked and Mother worked so there wasn't much excitement at our house. It was quiet and kind of lonely.

The spring of 1959 Jack and I decided that this was the year. We got engaged in 1954 and five years in the state of limbo was getting very close to being embarrassing. Jack had a good paying job, and I did, too. We were even getting along well! We had a little money saved for the wedding and honeymoon and to get set up in our first apartment. I had a hope chest full of dishes, linens, pans, blankets, lamps, and lots more. Girls did that in those days, in the 1950's. We were raised to be wives and mothers. We bought a few things here and there through our teen years, to bring to our marriages. Well, we really got into planning the wedding. We set the date for June 23, 1959. I bought a beautiful white lace dress and a beautiful headpiece and a veil with pearls on it. They were marked down but just what I wanted. Jack's sister Jane, who was my maid of honor, bought a coordinating pink lace dress. We picked out the flowers and of course, the ceremony would be at my little Baptist Church with our Minister officiating. We made reservations to go to Lake Okiboji in Northern Iowa, a beautiful clear blue lake for our honeymoon. We were so excited!

About a week before the big day, I think Jack's excitement turned to terror! I believe the boy got cold feet. My first inkling was when he bet our honeymoon money on a horse (a sure thing). The horse is still running I guess. Then he had to go to Household Finance and borrow $500.00 for our trip. His next subtle hint was when he didn't come home from his bachelor party for two days! I was beginning to get a little testy. However, we'd come this far- we were going to get married! The cake was decorated, the invitations were out, the flowers ordered, the apartment rented. On that June 23rd, we were going to get married.

Next Jack got-into an argument with his mother, of all things, and she wouldn't let his younger brothers and sisters come!! After those years of the kids planning to come and looking forward to our wedding, now they couldn't come!! By this time I was starting to squint my eyes, grit my teeth and mumble to myself a lot. I had set the wedding for a Tuesday night at 7:00 p.m. thinking that no one would be drinking and spoil things. That worked out fine, but what was I thinking of? These people didn't need to drink to create chaos. Jack's aunts were mad at him for arguing with his mother, so they sat across from the church honking and yelling "We're sorry to spoil your wedding!" They had promised to bring the lace table cloths, serving pieces and candelabras and sneakily just didn't bring them, The church loaned me some beautiful things in their place so there was no harm done.

I fixed Mom up so pretty. She had a new dress and a hat and gloves. I even made her wear a girdle though she really didn't need it. She insisted on wearing her underpants over it, I got ready at home - gown, shoes, veil, but surprise! the girl who came to drive me to the church drove Jack's convertible and guess what? The top wouldn't go up. So there we went. Driving down Broadway, top down, my veil blowing behind me in the breeze like Batman's cape!

Jack had chosen his Uncle Jim for his best man. Lord, why him?! Well, Uncle Jim in a tux is not a good thing. He was so enamored of himself all dressed up like that, wedding was not **on** his mind. He wanted to leave and party! Before the wedding we couldn't find him and he had the ring. There he was out behind the church in a mad embrace with my vocalist who was the Sunday school teacher's eighteen-year-old daughter. And Jim's wife sitting right there in the church!

Finally we got everyone in their places, the music was beautiful, we said our vows and were married. Despite all the complications it was beautiful to us. We were in love. We even managed to ignore the crazy honking aunts as we ran out of the church. The reception was nice, lots of good friends, our cake was beautiful and we got lots of lovely gifts. It was finally time to leave and someone piled the gifts in Jack's car. The one with the top that wouldn't go up. But wait, it was also the car with no keys. Uncle Jim had the keys last and they were in his pocket. But where was he? With that tux on he would probably be gone for three days. If we hurried maybe we could locate him. We got a ride to the closest phone which was in a dumpy little bar. In we all trudged. Gown, veil, tux, and all. Luckily we located Jim at the third bar we called. He brought us the keys, and back to the church we went. Luckily our wedding gifts hadn't been stolen from the convertible. We took them to Mom's house. Finally off on our Happy Honeymoon.

Our first stop was a town half way to the lake, Denison, Iowa. There was only one hotel in town and it looked just like the home of the Adam's family. An old lady with a flashlight and a cat took us up to our room. She turned the light switch on and an old ceiling fan came on that sounded like the propellers on a helicopter. The room was clean and the bed was comfortable, and so began our marriage. We got up, ate breakfast, and drove to the lake. It was truly beautiful.

There was a lot to do and we were having a great time. Except— someone had told us to use baby oil mixed with iodine for sun tan oil, and by the second day we were fried. I mean second or third degree burns. We couldn't walk or eat or wear clothes. We just lay there on the bed listening to Floyd Patterson lose the heavyweight boxing championship to Ingmar Johanson on the neighbor's radio. We were both delirious at times. I fell out of the bed once trying to reach a glass of water and cut my head. Blood was running in my eyes and face. All I could think of was if this was what I waited for all those years, then I want my Mother.

That's how we spent the last few days of our honeymoon. A neighbor came and put vinegar on us several times a day, God bless her. We got up stiff-legged, stiff-armed and we both walked like Frankenstein. I was still wearing my shorty nightgown and Jack had on his boxers. That's how we drove home. The top still didn't go up so we started real early before the sun got hot. I sure was glad to see mother when we pulled up at my house. But she was sobbing and crying. What was wrong? What now? She managed to get out between sobs, "I'm sorry I ruined your wedding. I wasn't going to tell you, but now I just have to."

Now I was really puzzled. What could sweet, plain quiet Mother have done? She answered, "I lost my panties in the receiving line." It was that darn tight girdle I had her wear. It had her held in so tiny that her big underpants just slid down to the floor!

"Mom, what did you do?" I asked her. "Oh," she said, "I just picked them up with my toe and stuck them in my purse, and kept right on shaking hands and greeting people."

Jack and I both comforted her and laughed so hard if we -hadn't been in such pain we would have rolled on the floor. So that was the start of our married life. And the marriage was like the wedding. Never a dull moment. Now don't you agree that my wedding was unique?

The Christmas Tree

Ramonia Evans

Truly, I've never had a Christmas that wasn't wonderful. Certainly, some have been much nicer, much happier than others, but each of them (and there have been a lot) have been special in their own way.

People always seem nicer and kinder to each other; smile more often and are friendlier. It's like we all have a big, happy secret that we share. I know it is fashionable, now, to be cynical, and focus on the commercialism of the holiday — the greed and selfishness that some display.

However, I believe these people are the minority. The child saving his pennies and nickels to buy his mom a pretty glass candy dish and Grandpa a fishing lure; the father working overtime to assure his children nice gifts under the tree and an extra nice Christmas dinner. The young mother cleaning her house spotless, studying recipe books, and writing Christmas cards late into the night, in preparation for her in-law's holiday visit. These things are done selflessly out of love. Most of us know the real reason for Christmas and are in awe of God's great gift to us of his Son. The birth of Baby Jesus. This is the inspiration for the generosity and love that is shown.

I grew up, my childhood was spent, in a small city in Iowa, Council Bluffs, where Christmas meant snow, sleds and reenacting the nativity with our Sunday school class at church each year. It meant bright blue skies by day, and at night skies of dark blue velvet, studded with diamonds and the moon so big and bright shining on us as Mother, my brother and I walked home from Christmas dinner at my Aunt Nina's house carrying our gifts that we couldn't help but be happy. All was right with our world.

We didn't have much materially as Mother had been left a widow when I was three, and my brother two, and she did washing for other people to support the three of us.

One of the treasures that I take out of what I call my "memory box" in my mind, to look at and enjoy, is the Christmas when I was five, about 1943 I guess.

It was the day before Christmas and as soon as we woke up, Mother called us into the front room. "Come see your surprise — the Christmas tree I decorated for you two last night. Tell me what you think." What we saw even to our young eyes was a very unusual Christmas tree, but we thought it looked great!

I smiled and told Mama "It looks pretty good for a homemade one." Mother's face fell. She had worked so hard to make us something lovely. Money was tight as usual, so she had walked up to the Christmas tree sales lot and gotten the branches that had broken off the trees. When she had them home, she made a skeleton frame of branches cut from the little elm tree behind our house, and filled it out with the fresh Douglas fir branches she had brought home. She finished it by hanging our few ornaments on the branches and the tinsel she saved from year to year.

Mother was so disappointed and thought her little tree a failure, because we knew it wasn't "store-bought". But we thought it was beautiful and loved it even more because she had made it for us and it was truly a gift of Christmas love.

I have had Christmases since that were much grander, with tall elegant trees. I've gotten gifts of pieces of furniture, a diamond ring, beautiful clothing, and sterling silver flatware. Two separate years I even had baby sons born December first as my Christmas surprise.

But I don't think I have ever had a happier, warmer, sweeter celebration of Jesus' birthday as we had in that little four room house by the railroad track.

I wish all of you an equally happy Christmas this year and always.

Ramona Evans
12/04/98

Who Do You Trust?

Ramona Bowen Evans

Francis came in the door from work and plopped down her purse. "What a crowd on that bus." she grumbled to her Mother, Sally. I had to stand all the way home and I was lucky to get a strap to hold on to. I wish those housewives could end their shopping sprees an hour or so earlier, so there would be room for a working girl to sit down.

As Francis kicked off her shoes, she noticed her Mother's guarded expression. "What are you doing Ma?" she asked, as she walked over o the table where her Mother sat writing and putting papers in envelopes. "Oh, no not again." "Ma, I have begged you not to send money to those TV preachers." For every one that is honest and sincere there are five shysters and charlatans." "You know your little pension barely meets your expenses, you hardly have enough left to buy stockings." Sally's voice was distressed, as she answered her daughter, "I know you don't approve, but I just feel a conviction to do this, I just feel that the Lord wants me to."

Francis saw it was no use to go through this, for the tenth time, but she grumbled to herself anyway, "Conviction, humph, the only conviction should be convicting those swindlers of fraud!" Especially that Oral Roberts, he even had to change his name, he was so sneaky. "Feather Dale Slater, her co-worker at the department store had told Francis that she had gone to school with him and he had gone by a different name, something that began with an R. Francis couldn't recall it, but now he was calling himself Oral – what was that all about? Francis put on her apron and went to fix their meager supper.

The ladies didn't know it then but that was the last time that scene was to be played. The next Monday when Francis went in to work, she along with all the other employees were given two week notices of termination. The department store was closing its doors forever. What would she do!!

Francis looked everywhere for another job with no luck. Sally didn't even have her stocking money to send to Mr. Roberts and his fellow beggars.

She prayed mightily about the situation, and then it came to her. She would ask the TV Evangelists to help her. Surely they would, just a little she would ask for, to ease them through this tight spot. After all, for years she'd been sending them money to help others.

Much cheered and relieved, Sally sat down and wrote nine sweet letters and posted them to her would-be saviors.

Francis was aghast at her Mother's plan when she heard about it, and had more that a little idea of how it would turn out. It turned out that Sally never heard one thing from any of them ever again. Not even to beg for money. She had been taken off the mailing lists, Francis figured. Sally was disillusioned and hurt.

Francis was angry, but glad to be rid of them. Then it came to her what Feather Dale had told her was Oral Roberts' real first name – Richtell (Rectal?)! And indeed he had turned out to be a real B—H—.

Francis found another job in a few weeks, as a receptionist and she even got to sit down and work. Sally began going to a little neighborhood church, where God was really at work, and the people there really loved her. Their lives were happy and peaceful, and the only dissent between them was whether to watch Lawrence Welk or Wagontrain...

Ramona Evans

02/22/96

About the Author's

The authors: Jessie Abbott is the oldest of the group. She is retired from the civil service and is eighty-five-years young. Romona Evans is a one of a kind Yankee who married a southerner. She has had many humorous episodes while here in the South. Betty Gallman, whose sense of humor, keeps everyone on their toes and laughing. Betty was stricken by polio when she was three years old. She never lets her disability slow her down. Bart Country was our mentor and our inspiration to write this book. Perry Woodley aka Woody is retired from the army. He was a POW in Korea and did three tours in Vietnam.

Printed in the United States
5053